Dmitry Bakin works as a chauffeur. He lives with his wife and son in Moscow.

Andrew Bromfield has translated widely from Russian, including *The Clay Machine-Gun*, *Omon Ra* and other novels by Victor Pelevin. He lives in Surrey.

DMITRY BAKIN

# Reasons
# for Living

*translated by*
*Andrew Bromfield*

**Granta Books**
London · New York

Granta Publications, 2/3 Hanover Yard, Noel Road, London N1 8BE

*Raisons de vivre* was first published by Editions Gallimard 1994
Published as *Strana proiskhozhdeniya* by Limbus Press 1996
First published in Great Britain by Granta Books 2002

A CIP catalogue record for this book is available from the British Library.

1 3 5 7 9 10 8 6 4 2

ISBN 1 86207 526 3

Typeset by M Rules

Printed and bound in Great Britain by Mackays of Chatham plc

# Contents

# Foreword

A book as finely and freshly written as this immediately attracts attention in literary Moscow. The networks buzz with questions and speculation. Who is Dmitry Bakin? 'The prose is stunning but what's his real name?' 'Must be X's son. I recognize some of the same turns of phrase.' 'No, X doesn't have a son. He's probably the critic Y's nephew, just changed his name slightly.' The mystery was compounded when Bakin did not appear to receive the 1996 Anti-Booker Prize for literature, a $10,000 award presented by Mikhail Gorbachev, but sent his wife instead, and even she disappeared as soon as the ceremonies ended. Any untoward efforts to identify, classify and explain away a talent as immediately classical in quality as it is elusive in personal origins came to naught.

As an American Slavist and translator I managed to win a professional entry to the puzzle, an introductory visit and interview with Dmitry Bakin, and apart from the lingering aura that emanates from a gifted artist, the mystery abated. The writer is a slender, wiry, thirty-something-year-old young man with a moustache and a bass voice. He lives in central Moscow in a pleasant, ordinary apartment. A gracious host, a responsible family man, somehow a southerner even as a Russian. He has strong and clear convictions – about politics and about literature. He's a conservative. While his young son scampers in and out and his wife cooks our supper, we talk a bit about him and literature, although he is not prone to literary chit-chat.

Here is the thumbnail biographical sketch that emerges from my interview.

Dmitry Gennadiyevich (his patronymic) was born in 1964 in Donetskaya oblast', which in fact is a southern province, and moved to Moscow when he was seven. He finished public school, then a year in medical training school (*uchilishche*), before doing his military service in the Soviet Army Medical Corps in 1984–6. He is positive about his experience in the army, considers it a rich time of learning and personal growth. According to Soviet laws of the time, a demobilized veteran was excused from the usual work requirements for up to a year, and Dmitry used that free time, exactly 364 days, to write some of the stories that form this collection. After that he got a job as a truck driver, and he continues in the profession now as a chauffeur. He decided against pursuing a university degree, although his first choice, had he taken that route, would have been medical school, not literary studies of any kind. Not only does his job as a driver provide him an income sufficient to support his family – his first priority – but he insists that in fact he happens to like the work. Writing must wait and find its place in his life in its own time. Words of praise and encouragement, even from his wife, do not persuade him that literature offers realistic prospects of financial support. For the foreseeable future, he says, he will work as a driver, feed his family and write only whenever he can.

Rather than publishing under his true last name, he chose Bakin as his *nom de plume*. There may be several reasons, but the chief one is to preserve his privacy in both worlds: he prefers his fellow drivers not to know him as a writer and fellow writers, with very few exceptions, not to know him at all. It's a way of distancing himself from the Russian literary world, a place, as he sees it, of politics, gossip and intrigues.

Two stories first appeared in 1989 in the popular magazine *Ogonyok* and then two more in the literary journal *Oktyabr'*. This collection was published in French by Gallimard in 1994, even before the Russian edition – *Strana proiskhozhdeniya* – in 1996. Since then he has published only two other short stories – 'The Lie's Guardian' (*Strazhnik lzhi*) in 1996 and 'The Tree's Son' (*Syn dereva*) in 1998, both in the leading literary journal *Znamia*.

The small quantity of Bakin's writing actually underscores its brilliant quality and makes it seem far more than merely 'promising'. Instead, it becomes something valuable in its own right, but fragile and special. The torrent of language sweeps the reader up into a stream of many levels. The sentences run on and spill over into eddies of modernism and more than any contemporaries, certainly in Russian writing today, one is reminded of Andrey Platonov; the great Russian prose writer of the early Soviet period soon repressed by the Stalinist machinery, now fully published and revered but still insufficiently read and recognized in the West. Platonov is the primary modern poet-in-prose of the Russian village as the repository of an alternative consciousness, one that precedes those rationalistic philosophies that would generalize and conceptualize the human being, erase his individual features and diminish his ancient drive for freedom. Stylistically, in its rush of metaphors and merging voices polished and overlaid by a remote, impersonal narrator – even in its rhythm – Bakin's prose reminds one of Platonov's writing.

Other comparisons might be possible: Gogol, in the seemingly spontaneous flow of language and surprising turns it takes; Chekhov, in the inherent, holistic sympathy Bakin shows to his own characters; Andrey Bely, in the depiction of obsessive visions; Boris Pilnyak, in the neo-primitivism that permeates his narrative voice. But essentially Bakin's voice doesn't seem at all derivative. For all his verbal intricacies, rhetorical discipline and refined tropes, an authentic passion rushes in and gives his prose tactile values and a sensuality that is muted, even surreptitious, but unmistakably present. Within a few pages the reader starts to care about the characters encountered, their past, their pain, their quirks, their shining delusions – or are they truly visions? The contagion may come from the characters themselves, who care strongly about each other in mainly spiritual ways.

Faulkner comes to mind, and in fact Bakin himself brings his name up frequently in conversation. There are affinities in Bakin's characters' concern with genealogy and decline, even decay, as time inexorably and mysteriously makes its way through the mortal cells that hope to obstruct it. As in Faulkner, remote historical events, brutal and traumatic, become mythicized, then personalized and finally, when no recourse is left, poeticized. Gabriel García Márquez, himself a Faulknerian in early inspiration, is not a writer that Bakin mentions, but an analogy with *One Hundred Years of Solitude* and other early works certainly seems possible. One finds it in the visions that well up in his characters' consciousness, in the elaborate dreams and metaphors for the perceptions of reality that drive their actions.

Bakin's language surges powerfully forward, running in several channels simultaneously. It is at times primitivistic in its expressive repetitions, at others imagistic in its wealth of metaphor, and of course there is a realistic matrix to his narrative threads. These are no sketches or prose poems. Told here are actual stories with interconnecting lines of suspense and meaning. But there are also great mute gaps in narrative chronologies, untold passages that remain for the reader to surmise. His stories' crucial events belong mainly to a relatively distant past, full of force and violence, but Bakin transforms them for the reader through the subtly changing light of his expression. His peculiarly ornate linguistic veil changes these solitary characters from their utterly ordinary surroundings and painful solitude into archetypes whose suffering transcends the local village and rises, like the smoke from Bedolagin's body as it burns with the gathered leaves in 'Leaves' (List'ya), to a purely spiritual dimension with implicitly universal human contours.

Bakin's people are contradictory, as if compelled by unknown antediluvian sources to act out the identities assigned them by the fusing forces of history, myth and individual consciousness. Afflicted or even marked by some absent God, the primary character that dominates each story may be essentially negative in the assertion of a stubborn will, but also thoroughly persuasive as a convincing character, like the cruel patriarch Krainov in the story 'The Surveyor' (Zemlemer), or the riddle-like stranger who carries in a tobacco pouch a lock of hair from a child named Idea and in his heart a bullet, in 'Country of Origin' (Strana proiskhozhdeniya). Character, myth and language are the three primary components of Bakin's prose, but language dominates the other two and merges them all into an integrated whole voice.

Almost no one writes like this today, at least not in Russia, nor in America for that matter. At a time when postmodern satire has established itself as the strongest literary mode, with talents such as Victor Pelevin capturing younger readers and the conceptualist Vladimir Sorokin establishing a small following among the critical older intelligentsia, Bakin's writing reasserts a healthy diversity in Russian literature and makes important reconnections with the Russian modernism brutally cut down by Stalin and his doctrines. More fundamentally, especially for non-Russian readers, it speaks of a renewal of the great Russian literary heritage of passionate concern for the easily overlooked little person in a harsh social climate and for the magic of good writing that dramatizes the single individual's fate. One can only hope that Bakin continues to write such poignant, powerful stories. With this small book he has established his own talent's authenticity, one that adds a vibrant new voice to the ever resonant legacy of Russian prose. English-language readers are fortunate to have access to it now in Andrew Bromfield's translation.

Byron Lindsey, May 2002

# Translator's Note

The task of translating the stories of Dmitry Bakin and producing a text which effectively conveys his style in English requires the resolution of certain specific difficulties. Bakin does not write in simple literary narrative Russian prose. He has a manner that is quite individual, frequently employing long, rolling periods within which the boundary between narrative and direct speech is often blurred. In combination with numerous metaphors and some non-standard elements of syntax, this frequently tends to produce an incantatory effect. In other words, he is not an 'easy' author.

The historical and social context of these stories is broadly post-World War II Russia (Soviet Union), and where this is not specifically stated it is clearly implied (no more is necessary for the Russian reader) in the text, such as the mention of the twenty-year state loan bonds in 'The Surveyor', or the details of

Soviet army life in 'Hare's Eye' – these examples could be multiplied to produce a lengthy list. This context, which is of considerable interest in itself, is inevitably largely alien to the twenty-first-century English reader and in a few cases it has been felt necessary to clarify certain Soviet realia. This is intended to serve the same purpose in the transition from Russian to English as the 'smoothing out' of certain elements of Bakin's distinctive patterns of punctuation.

The stories do not, however, make their initial impact at the level of socio-historical context (which is entirely absent in the case of 'Armed Defence'). They deal with modes of being and experiencing. The efforts of the translator and editors have therefore been primarily directed to producing an English text which conveys the distinctiveness of Bakin's voice, its sweep and force, its variety of registers, ranging from the vatic and riddling to the most brutally lucid.

Readers with a specialist interest may well spot elements in this voice and 'literary worldview' which link Bakin to certain identifiable strands in Russian and Soviet literature. No specialist knowledge should be required, however, to appreciate the intensity with which that vision is expressed here.

# Leaves

He arrived in the village as a twelve-year-old boy, from the direction of the open field, so that the river was on his left and the forest on his right, and before entering the village he walked through the unfenced graveyard along a pathway strewn with river sand, and his bare feet, insensitive to the sharp stones and broken glass, sensed the perennial chill of the earth. He crossed a patch of wasteland and passed by the house at the edge of the village without knocking, because he knew that people who live at the edge of villages are surly and rough and ready to take flight, passed by the second house because it was too big, passed by the rubble of the third house, and in the fourth house he was taken in by a dirty one-armed man and a sturdy half-blind woman who had been waiting for the arrival of Jesus Christ for seventeen childless years. For some time they looked at him without speaking, then they went into the next room and talked about something in low voices, then they came back. The one-armed man sat down at the table and the woman stood to one side and looked at the wall. The man asked, 'Where are you from?' He said nothing, staring at the man's chest. The man said, 'You were born in this house before the war.' He stared at the man's chest and said, 'No.' The man raised his hand and pointed with his forefinger in the direction of an unmade bed, 'Right there.' He said, 'No.' The man said darkly, 'You were born twelve years ago, you were born in August.' The woman, still looking at the wall, said, 'On the first Sunday in September.' The man turned his stiff, intense face to look at her and worked his jaw, then turned back and said, 'In September.' He said, 'No.' The man stood up and said, 'Full stop.'

Next morning he was washed, his hair was trimmed, he was fed nettle soup and nailed tight to the surname of Bedolagin. He tried three times to run away from the house of the one-armed man and the half-blind woman, and three times he was caught, twice in the forest, where he ate snails after the rain, searching them out under the stones or pulling them off the wet stumps and roots, and once at the railway station where he was waiting for a train and hadn't noticed that the rails had been dismantled. He didn't try to run away any more after that, he did everything they asked without saying a word, carefully avoiding looking anyone in the face. One time the one-armed man said, 'He's ashamed of us.' But the woman said that it was resignation.

When the German prisoners-of-war laid the rails on new wooden sleepers and reinforced the embankment where it had been damaged by the bombs and escape was open to everyone, the one-armed man died. Before he died he hadn't risen from his bed for two weeks, except for the rare occasions when he went outside to relieve himself, which only happened very rarely as death approached because he didn't eat or drink anything. Under the two blankets and the greatcoat turned rusty by the damp, under the taut mantle of his withered skin, his bones felt neither heat nor cold. That was when he told the woman that a man feels heat and cold with his bones, feels hunger and heat with his bones. He didn't say another word, because he had every right to forget the meaning of all words. Guided by those who had died long before, he put every cell in his body at the service of a craving for death, refusing the medicines and healing infusions which the woman tried to pour into him during his moments of oblivion.

Bedolagin-junior sat in the corner still feeling like a stranger, and for the first time since he had come to this village from the direction of the open field and entered this house, he looked openly, without hiding his eyes, at the half-blind woman and the one-armed man who was dying. The woman said something to the man in a dull, muffled voice that sounded measured and unhurried like the chiming of a clock, and then realized he wouldn't answer, because he no longer understood human speech. She straightened up, slowly moved away from the bed and looked at Bedolagin-junior. He looked straight into her face and her eyes, for he already knew he would stay in this house for ever and take the one-armed man's place, according to the unwritten earthly law by which life occupies the space freed by death and is buried beneath its own inheritance.

When Bedolagin-junior became simply Bedolagin, who looked at people openly, he didn't go to the graveyard to which the one-armed man was carried off on the crest of a wave of solitary keening after the old woman who lived at the edge of the village had washed him and shaved him and powdered his cheeks with a red flower's pollen. But those who carried the one-armed man and those who followed the coffin were unable to rid themselves of the conviction that he was following them, hiding in the gateways, running from one tree to another, from one house to another and then hiding behind the gravestones and watching as they buried the dead man. Sitting at the table in the Bedolagins' house on the day of the wake, drunk from moonshine and malnutrition, the old woman who lived at the edge of the village sang paeans of praise to the one-armed man, twisting and squirming on her chair like a small whirlwind of dust and ashes, barely even keeping her balance and looking at Bedolagin-junior, who was sitting opposite her, with her dehydrated brown eyes gleaming like polished wood, and she said, 'Behold the fruit,' and she said, 'Of the dead seed.' She was the first to get up and start to take her leave. In her movements there was no trace of the sense of doom that appears in people's movements a long time before they even grow old. But still no one dared to touch her, afraid she might crumble into dust like an ancient vase that has lain on the bottom of the ocean for centuries in a motionless solution of water, salt and time, and they took leave of her only with their eyes, the way people take leave of a mirage.

In the summer of the year when the one-armed man died and word came that the war was over in the west but not in the east, and long troop-trains carried the bodies and souls of soldiers still capable of fighting right across the country, with the military matériel that had survived the battles loaded on steel platforms, while hospital trains carried the eyes of the deafened, the ears of the blinded, the mute lowing of those who had been struck dumb, the thirst of men wounded in the belly, for whom the war was over once and for all, the women of the village, driven by hunger, gathered up their knapsacks, their bundles and their bags and set out in the direction of Kherson, where they hoped to exchange those of their belongings the Germans had left untouched for seeds, pipes and domesticated birds and animals. A few cripples demobilized at the beginning of the war, a few shell-shock victims and the married fool who had an army ticket instructing him to stay put stood in the middle of the dead field and watched as the heavily loaded women trudged along the white, dusty road, past the pine forest and the church on the hill, and then disappeared round the bend, and not one of them believed they would come back, they were convinced that the white dusty road was that very road which you can walk along for ever and disappear without trace, vanish into thin air. In the village the men went back to their houses, cursing their infirmity, fastening all the locks, latches and bolts on their doors in the hope of shutting themselves away from the world where the women had vanished into thin air and disappeared without trace; they surrounded themselves with bottles, demijohns, buckets and petrol-cans of moonshine, laying them out to define the orbit of their domain, and then sank beneath the heavy rolling waves of drunkenness, falling asleep in order to seek for an answer, convinced that everything they saw in their dreams had to be believed, for reality is only half of the truth and people have nowhere else to seek the other half except in their dreams. And so, having constructed for themselves the prison cells and dungeons required for the search for truth, they lived behind the bars of their own incapacity for two weeks, and during that time they wallowed in fruitless vacillation, sprawling under the table in their own vomit, among the gobs of spittle, saliva-soaked dog-ends and lumps of clay from their boots; enveloped in the dense gloom of no-man's land; having forgotten the name of what it was they were searching for.

Meanwhile the children, granted total freedom, disappeared into the forest from dawn to dusk during the long summer days, where they searched for ruined, buried trenches and abandoned dugouts, scampered about in the narrow space of the earth, risking burial alive by the rotten beams, stumbling across jagged fragments of shrapnel, rusty towbars, half-decayed groundsheets and metal yokes, hoping to find weapons and ammunition that they could explode in the flames of their campfire.

At the beginning of the third week the women returned, harnessed into the shoulder-straps of their knapsacks and bags, and in the yards they discovered dogs dying of hunger and cats run wild and dishevelled crows sitting on the roofs of the houses. The fool's wife came into their yard, dragging in after her a skinny, dirty goat, which from the look of it anyone would have said was dead, if it hadn't actually been moving its legs. She tied it to the fence and trudged wearily over to the house, but the door was locked from the inside. She hammered on the door with her hands, her feet, the handle of a spade, the head of an axe and stones, she charged the door at a run with her shoulder and called out in a terrible, quivering voice. She was getting ready to take out the window-panes when the door creaked open and a face as yellow as sand, unshaven and twisted out of shape by astonishment, appeared and fixed her with crazy, staring eyes like the eyes of the wild cats that watched her go by as she walked through the village to her home. The hair dangled down over the yellow face, and the ears sticking out at its sides were stopped up with grey pus mixed with blood. It took her a long time to recognize this otherworldly being as her own crazy husband, who clasped her in his arms and collapsed on the doorstep with his face buried in her skirt, dribbling and muttering about the sacred indissolubility of marriage. Then she gave a hollow groan and said, 'My God,' and she said, 'Damn you, you son of a bitch,' and again she said, 'My God.' She helped him to his feet and led him into the house, where hundreds of green and black flies were buzzing around above the broken stools and smashed bottles and the old daguerrotypes of relatives who died during the previous century that had been trampled underfoot.

She said, 'My God, O my God,' and she said, 'God, make me a widow,' and she said, 'Damn you, you bastard, you bastard.' Much the same thing was taking place in the other houses of the village, where the men had been dragged out of their noxious miasma by the ears and were being washed and dressed in clean clothes, stoned with the stones of curses and beaten about the face, and everything capable of clouding the faculty of reason, even soured apples, was instantly hidden away or ruthlessly destroyed, and as the dark spheres of the days rolled by the women, having expelled or displaced the intoxicating poison, compelled their men to believe that they were the truth the men had been stubbornly seeking as they lay sprawled under the table in their own vomit among the gobs of spittle and saliva-soaked dog-ends, enveloped in the dense gloom of their no-man's land.

Bedolagin took no part in the games organized by his peers who wished to tempt fate and he became even more withdrawn, preferring the inner life to the outer; the roads he followed to the illusory goals which would satisfy his thirst for understanding were all roads that led away from them. They called him across when he was standing in the long, hungry queue in front of the single-storey wooden-plank barracks where the bread and soap was delivered, and he followed them. They stopped at the back wall of the barracks and laughed as they showed him a crack between the warped boards and said to him, 'Go on, take a look.' He bent down to look through the crack and saw the murky, dusty, shop storeroom, sacks of flour, sacks of bread and on the sacks the manager of the shop had pushed the sales assistant down on her back and was pulling up her skirt, and the resistance she offered was like the resistance of water to a swimmer who wants to swim too fast. Bedolagin couldn't see her face, but from the way her body was shaking he realized she was laughing, and then the manager of the shop unbuttoned his trousers and climbed on top of her. Bedolagin straightened up and they looked at him, laughing. One said, 'What a rogue, eh?' Another said, 'If we gave them a good fright now, they'd never get unstuck, like dogs.' A third said, 'Like railway trucks.' The leader said, 'He should go,' and he said to Bedolagin, 'You go, he'll get down off her soon and she'll open the shop.' Another said, 'You'll get to see plenty more, they're always at it.'

They brought him to a school that smelled of horses, where he wrote down what they dictated to him between the lines of newspapers and sang in a choir under a huge portrait of a man with squinting, domineering eyes. The music teacher smashed a ruler as heavy as a traffic-boom down on to the skull of anyone who failed to shut his trap at the same time as everyone else.

In the autumn they were taken to the common and they gathered up the fallen leaves with home-made wooden rakes and brooms, raking them into large loose heaps which grew bigger and darker from one day to the next and then, when the trees had finished dropping their leaves and stood quite naked, they set the leaves on fire and their clothes smelled of the acrid smoke until winter.

During the misty days the half-blind woman went out into the fields to glean ears of grain at the risk of ending up behind bars for ten years, and while she crawled on all fours over the black ploughland with its sprinkling of hoarfrost, Bedolagin hid behind the railway embankment and watched to make sure the collective farm warden didn't suddenly appear on his horse. Then she would give him a sign and he would walk along the embankment to the bridge, his fear preventing him from feeling the freezing cold, and they would meet, pale and dirty, under the bridge and she would say, 'Why, the bastards,' and he would say,

'Never mind.' She would say, 'Why, the bastards,' and keep on saying it all the way home.

But everywhere, no matter where he might be, his dominant urge was to stand aside, unmoving, from the turbid torrent of the years in which people went hurtling along towards perfection among silt, broken branches, threadbare clothes, twisted guns and the bones tumbled smooth by the water, to stand aside and give them advice, cheating the shadow of the law that fell across the head of each of them from the moment they were born.

In time his thoughts and desires changed, filling his head with women of every shade and hue; they loved him and they called to him, but he didn't know the road that led to them. In hopes of finding the road he listened to the old woman who lived at the edge of the village, who would often come to their house in the evening and sit at the table rocking to and fro on her chair, barely keeping her balance, as she had five years before at the one-armed man's wake. He'd realized a long time ago that she lingered here on earth as an instrument of the dead, and the dead spoke through her lips in order to warn the living of things that remained unclear during life, and she would prophesy in a hoarse, croaking, icy voice through the wheezing in her chest and her throat, through her coughing, sneezing and runny nose, about what to do to avoid dying of hunger. 'To one bucket of water,' she said, 'add one spoonful of bran, two sprats and goosefoot'; how to avoid getting pregnant, how to deliver a child, what to feed goats in winter, how to treat tuberculosis and dysentery. Bedolagin pretended to be asleep that evening when twenty-five-year-old Anna was thrown out of her home for all the wild nights she'd spent with her collection of men and came to their house, where she found the old woman, the half-blind woman and a French marquise who had emigrated from France at the beginning of the century engaged in conversation. After a little while the old woman said to her, 'A woman who goes from less to more and from more to even more will end up making do with the very least, because there'll always be lots of things she won't be able to fit in.' Anna said, 'No.' The half-blind woman said, 'Quiet.' The old woman said, 'He's sleeping.' Anna said, 'He's not sleeping.' The marquise said, 'At twenty-five all women are fallen women.' The old woman said, 'He who gave us life will not forgive.' Anna said, 'No one gave us life, we're the products of an explosion.'

He was sleeping when the colonel of the shadow forces came to their house late one evening to settle his own fate, a tall, morose middle-aged man who had liberated the village from the Germans a year before Bedolagin-junior was declared Bedolagin and first felt the weight of the curses of family and inheritance. But this was no longer the same artillery colonel the village remembered from when he was quartered with the Bedolagins, the colonel who bounded out on to the porch with his face grey from sleepless fury when poor targeting led to three fighters dotted with red stars strafing the liberated village and a column of his soldiers, together with their horses, wagons and field guns, the colonel who stretched out his massive hands towards the sky and the planes with his spread fingers crooked as though he wanted to reach out and grab them, drag them down and break them across his knee. That colonel had strained his innards to breaking as he yelled and yelled, 'What're you firing at! Cease fire! It's us down here! It's us! Wave the flag at them!' That colonel had wept, but kept on shouting hoarsely like a tuneless instrument being tuned and many of them had seen the blood come pouring out of his throat and seen him tumble down from the porch, clutching at the banisters. The soldiers had picked that colonel up, put him in a cart, covered him with sackcloth and borne him off to do battle. The colonel who came back late one evening six years and two months later had left the first colonel behind in the cart, covered with sackcloth impregnated with the stench of corpses, or somewhere on one of the twists of the spiral leading him upwards into the darkness. More like a prostitute than a soldier, unable to see any way out except marriage, unpredictable in his actions, with a face frozen in the paralysis of responsibility, he came into the house when Bedolagin was sleeping and told the half-blind woman to gather her things, and told her many other things as well. In the morning the half-blind woman told Bedolagin that she was leaving. She spoke for a long time in the dull, muffled voice she'd used for talking to the one-armed man when he had cast off the burden of understanding. Bedolagin asked, 'How did he know your husband had died?' She looked at the wall and said, 'I wrote to him,' and she said, 'He says you're to come with us.' He asked, 'Where to?' She said, 'To Moscow.' He said, 'I won't go.' She said, 'I knew you wouldn't.' The colonel came in and said it was time to go to town to see the notary. Bedolagin said, 'Get out.' The colonel went out without a word. The half-blind woman said, 'You're just a snivelling kid.' He said, 'This is my home.' They went to town, bought some vodka and went to the notary, where the half-blind woman registered a deed of gift and some other documents according to which, when Bedolagin came of age, which was due to happen in three months, he acquired the rights of a householder. Just before they left the colonel said to him, 'Sooner or later everything that exists ceases to exist, and then something comes along to take its place, but not always something better,' and they went away. Then Bedolagin did what the cripples and shell-shock victims did when the women, driven by hunger, had trudged away along the white dusty road and disappeared without trace, vanished into thin air. He sat for an hour facing the empty half-litre bottle, thinking about deliverance and longing for the warmth of his mother's womb, and then, staggering and hiccupping, he went out into the yard, intending to inspect the lightest and most insubstantial part of his inheritance, which consisted of three buildings: the house with an adjacent summer kitchen, a shed blackened by the rain which, strictly speaking, was not a shed, but more like a lean-to for storing firewood, and a cellar. He wandered between the apple and plum trees, and counted the vegetable plots planted with beetroot and potatoes. Staggering into the summer kitchen at the sound of a rat's squeal he turned over saucepans, mixing bowls and chafing dishes and spotted two kitbags left by the colonel, in which he found a dozen dark-green cans of meat paste, bars of chocolate, hard tack and cans of stewed beef covered with a layer of grease, as well as soldier's underwear, an officer's pea jacket, a pair of officer's boots and new puttees.

In the morning he felt worse than he ever had, except for the moment of his birth. A cat attached itself to him and lived in the house for a day and a night, leaving behind fleas and a strong smell. He went to the old woman who lived at the edge of the village and asked what he should do if he had fleas in the house and she said, 'Pick plenty of wormwood and spread it on the floor,' and then she said, 'Don't let cats in the house.' He picked plenty of wormwood and spread it on the floor.

A week later Anna came to see him and entered the room where Bedolagin was sitting surrounded by dried-out worm-wood and anti-tank trenches, camouflage nets and barricades created by his drunken imagination in order to protect the house against infiltration by cats, finishing off the last but one of the bottles of home brew that had been in the half-blind woman's larder and were intended for the old woman who lived at the edge of the village and for the French marquise who had emi-grated from France at the beginning of the century. He lifted his head and gazed through a transparent, impenetrable wall of drunken alienation at the twenty-five-year-old woman, who walked over to him across the crunching wormwood and, gazing into his eyes, flicked him with her finger so that it hurt, so that he leapt back away from her into the corner. And then he felt the impenetrable, transparent wall built to withstand a meteorite shower crack apart and crumble to dust at a single flick of a woman's fingers, leaving him naked, defenceless and pitiful, dumped back into the turbid torrent of time in which people went hurtling along towards perfection among silt, broken branches, threadbare clothes, twisted guns and bones tumbled smooth by the water. She said, 'They've thrown me out of the house.' That was what she said and a fatal, demonic smile played about her lips. He said, 'I see.' She said, 'I wanted to spend the night here.' That's what she said. He said, 'Listen, you know where you can . . .' She said, 'Honest to God, I've nowhere to spend the night.' That's what she said. He said, 'Okay.' She said, 'Thank you.' That's what she said, and she laughed. He looked and said, 'If you laugh once more I'll punch your face in. If you're still in my house at seven o'clock in the morning I'll punch your face in.' That's what he said, because he couldn't wait to get back to restoring the transparent, impenetrable wall that had shattered at a single flick of her fingers.

Of course, she came to him in the night; he heard the worm-wood crunching under her bare feet, and instead of punching her face in he said, 'There are fleas here, they're everywhere.' She said, 'If there are fleas, they're always everywhere.' He said, 'They're everywhere.' She said, 'Never mind,' and she asked, 'How old are you? Seventeen?' He said, 'Maybe I'm fifty, but they said I was seventeen.' She said, 'That's enough idle chatter.' And she bombarded him with barrages of fire and the blasts of sound-less explosions such as no raw recruit at the front line or any dead man in the furnace of a crematorium had ever endured; her lips, arms, breasts and legs stung him with electricity; she summoned up the earthquake and the scalding wind, transforming their bodies into molten lava, and blinding light alternated with stifling, clammy darkness; she did whatever she wanted with him, and he thought this must be how the universe was created.

In the morning she left and as he watched her go he thought: She'll come back. He didn't clear away the withered wormwood from the floor for a month, expecting to wake up in the night and hear crunching footsteps and see her fatal smile in the dark-ness of his anticipation. Then the wormwood turned to dust and he was forced to clear it away, because mice had appeared in the house and he often took the rustling of the mice at night for the light step of a woman's bare feet. Soon after that he and the rest of the village learned that Anna had gone away to the city with a tall, handsome man. But the news barely even shook Bedolagin's faith in her return. As he weeded the neglected kitchen garden and spread dried manure on the vegetable patches he muttered to himself, 'Who gives a damn about the city, and whatever bastard built it?' But after he'd kept his hopes alive for a year and a half, the day dawned when he stood in the garden with an axe in his hand and looked at his house, warmed by nothing but the ashes of faith, and he felt an urge to maim, annihilate, smash, and that day he let drop the nails out of his hands and said, 'I'm just a stupid fool, and she's a foul whore . . .'

In his craving for stillness and silence, he pursued a direct, undeviating course to his cross, which excluded any halts in havens of light and joy along the way, with the result that once again a wall grew up between him and the world. His imagina-tion was obsessed by the delusion of being outside time, and the power that had led every cell in the one-armed man's body to extinction and death infected his blood, moving his arms, feet and neck, drying his throat and sharpening his vision with a hopeless clarity. If he got drunk in the house no one saw him, but if he got drunk in the garden many of them saw him and they saw the straight, undeviating line of the course he had taken, which only appeared crooked and twisted from the outside, they saw him sprawling in the puddles under the railway embankment or with his head parting the mud in the gutter and his backside jutting up in the air. A pregnant cat that leapt the anti-tank trenches and penetrated the barricades and saw right through the camouflage nets came to him in his dreams, sinking the needles of its teeth into his scrotum, and he smashed it against all the signposts along the path he followed back to the wasteland of wakening; the next night a snake bit him in the palm of the hand that he had raised over a crowd of people as he bade them go down on their knees, and his hand fell on the crowd, crushing it with the weight of its sudden swelling.

The old woman who lived at the edge of the village bunched together the fingers that refused to obey her, and wrote a letter to the half-blind woman, insisting that she must come, but the half-blind woman was unable to come because of some illness.

The colonel came. But he was no longer the colonel who once fought a war, or the colonel who came to the village to carry off the half-blind woman and crown her head with the wedding garland that had bowed her down to the ground. Grown hopelessly overweight, like someone half bound and tied he struggled to drag his body along, like the horse that had dragged along the cart with that other colonel covered by the sackcloth. His face, as dark as a secret, was only rarely split in two by a smile, whenever he suddenly recalled the requirements of etiquette. The colonel took a bottle of vodka and several tins of food out of his case;

they drank the vodka, the colonel gave his driver money and the driver brought another three bottles; they sat at the table and the driver slept in the car; the colonel smoked, shaking the ash into a green-tarnished shell-case from a large-calibre machine-gun. The colonel said that the half-blind woman would come as soon as she was back on her feet and he said, 'She misses you a lot.' Bedolagin said, 'Tell her I miss her a lot too.' Bedolagin looked at the colonel and felt the light and pattern of the world crumble into atoms and sounds scatter into the air, and the colonel's voice was like the rustling of sand. And then the colonel got up and put on his greatcoat and Bedolagin went on sitting at the table, and the colonel told him not to see him off and said he should go to bed, and ponderously, making what seemed to be an immense effort, he set off out of the house without pausing in the doorway or on the porch from which he'd fallen seven years earlier with the blood gurgling in his throat.

Bearing in mind what the colonel of the shadow forces had said about a minimal subsistence income and also the fact that living alone and outside the law cost money, after changing his mind a few times Bedolagin took a job in the maternity department of the red-brick hospital close to the forest, where for two months and four days he kept his teeth gritted and his nostrils plugged up with putty, as he trudged sullenly across the overshadowed yard, dragging a squeaky, rotten old trolley loaded with sheets and pillowcases taken from under women giving birth in response to encouragement from the post-war government. In the laundry located in the basement of a grey building fifty metres from the morgue he offloaded his bundle of dirty laundry on to the floor, lifting each sheet with a finger and thumb and counting out loud as he dropped them at the feet of a gaunt man with a curved spine who was as indifferent to the mind-searing stench as though every day he clambered back into the place from which he had appeared in the world and lived there. In the evening, when the matron poured Bedolagin a glass of medical spirit, he would say to her, 'That's no way to live, that's the wrong place.' At the end of July, as he was counting out the sheets in front of the apathetic curved man, he said, 'This is my last trolley.' The curved man grinned, stuffed the sheets and the pillowcases into a blanket-cover, slung it over his shoulder and carried it off to the washerwoman. Bedolagin went outside and walked around the village for a long time, gritting his teeth, with the putty in his nostrils, then he pulled out the putty, climbed over the fence of someone else's garden and slumped silently into a bed of roses.

He lasted even less time as a guard on a goods train than he did as a labourer in the maternity section of the red-brick hospital, his career numbering only the seventeen days required for the journey to Rostov and back, because on the very first night his partner suggested he might play the woman's part, only backside frontwards, and for seventeen days with murder in mind he kept a tight grip on his monkey-wrench, not wanting to play the man or the woman, as dumb as a clam with speechless fury, and all the time still pursued inexorably by the smell of nascent life.

He went back to the cold house, firmly determined to rid himself of all witnesses to his life, and he locked himself away inside its four walls, at the age of twenty having suffered and accepted a wound which the old woman who lived at the edge of the village said she saw in her morning visions, streaked across with spasms of orange pain, but thanks to her prayers and chanting and spells they merged together and melted away, and he saw that the shed for firewood was almost empty, with nothing left but kindling soaked through by the dampness of the autumn rains that had pounded the old, thin tarpaper of the roof to pieces and washed the waterproof tar off the lean-to, and standing in the orchard under the black apple tree that had twined its roots around the grave of his hopes, he sensed that even after another hundred years he would still be arriving in the village over and over again as a twelve-year-old boy, eternally repeating himself, striving to grind himself into dust as he travelled along the furrow of Central Russia, in a cold autumn, from the direction of the open field, so that the river would always be on his left and the forest on his right and his bare feet, insensitive to the sharp stones and broken glass, would sense the perennial chill of the earth.

So he went to the old woman who lived at the edge of the village and asked: How should I live, what should I be? But every autumn the old woman's brain turned to dry ice, her heart beat once a day, her tongue, forgotten by the dead, would not move, the streams of light from the window poured into her soul through her eyes and for those eyes everything except the light was worthless dust. Like the old woman who lived at the edge of the village, the marquise who had emigrated from France at the beginning of the century didn't give advice in autumn, but she suggested he should get a job as a stoker at the school because, she said, it would soon be winter, and she said, 'It's time to burn the trees.' He was told the same thing by Anna's father after he helped him saw down an overgrown willow on the common, and he said, 'All right,' and then he asked, 'Does Anna write home?' Anna's father gave him a sideways glance and said she did, and asked, 'Why?' He said, 'No reason,' and he asked, 'Will she come to the village?' Anna's father said, 'No.' He asked, 'Why?' Anna's father said, 'Because I'd kill her.'

Late in September he went to the headmaster of the school and said he was willing to work as a stoker in the boiler-room; the headmaster asked whether he was willing to work at night;

he said he was. He was directed by the headmaster to the north wing of the building, where he went down the steps into the basement and found himself in a cramped, stifling space where he saw a long, soot-blackened bench, a lopsided black table, an open cast-iron furnace with its flap hanging on a single hinge, a large boiler and rusty pipes through which the hot steam circulated; one corner of the boiler-room was screened off with three broad planks held upright by stakes driven into the ground and behind them shovels and black, battered buckets lay on a heap of coal, and at the height of a man's head there was a railway spike driven into the wall with a kerosene lamp hanging on it bound round with copper wire that the damp air had turned green, and for a brief moment, as he gazed into the fire, he felt he'd reached the final goal of his journey. Sitting on the bench was a red-haired man with a face covered in grime. His powerful shoulders filled up all the space from the cast-iron furnace to the opposite wall, seeming to be much broader than the length of the table, and it was as though the building had coalesced with the solid darkness behind his back and was supported on his shoulders, and if he should suddenly decide to get up, then the entire school would rise up along with him, ripped away from its foundations. When Bedolagin entered the boiler-room not a single movement stirred on the face with the large nose, the lips clamped as tight as a vice and the massive chin protruding like the chin of a bull chewing the cud, as though the crust of coal dust and soot had entirely paralysed the nerves to the muscles of the forehead, cheeks and lips. For a split second the eyes stared hard at Bedolagin, then their gaze drifted off and away into the distance, just as though someone had thrown a cobblestone into a river, hoping to block its path to the ocean. Bedolagin stood in front of him for a long time, unable to decide whether he was hopelessly drunk or gripped by some extreme lethargy, and he'd already made up his mind to leave when the red-headed man's chin suddenly quivered as though a stratum of rock had slipped and split away, and the impact of the internal shock shattered the rigidity of the face, making it seem it must inevitably crumble into a shower of black stones, like the wall of a house destroyed by a blow from within, and through the distinct booming of the blood in his ears Bedolagin heard a voice filled with hatred for itself saying, 'Have you ever seen six toes on the same foot?'

Afterwards, during the autumn evenings when they sat on the long, smoke-blackened bench, dappled by the coloured light from the flames in the cast-iron furnace, he never told Bedolagin that he felt any pain or suffered from any feeling of inferiority, which would only have been natural if he had four toes instead of the five decreed by God; endowed with a ferocious intransigence and a monstrous strength which had often served to assert his own correctness, he refused point-blank to accept that he was a freak of nature, realizing in the depths of his heart that that merely demeaned a man, but did not justify him, as Bedolagin supposed. A year earlier, when the sixth toe was merely hinted at in a pale wart beside the big toe of his left foot, and the doctor from the big red-brick hospital had said that it was a callus and prescribed looser-fitting shoes, the old woman who lived at the edge of the village had advised him to remember all his sins and repent and said, 'If that doesn't help, thank God the horn has grown on your foot and not on your head,' hinting by her words that women had been unfaithful to him, which drove him into a terrible fury and led him to drop his trousers in front of her and ask what else these blasted women needed, after which the old woman was unable to close her mouth for three hours, and then only after she pricked herself in the ear with a needle to relieve the cramp in her jaws. But even despite their obvious absurdity the woman's words became firmly fixed in his head and he turned the gloomy frenzy with which he had sought a means to rid himself of the sixth toe to searching for the cause of its appearance.

Moved by sympathy and fear, Bedolagin went to the hospital and asked them to cut off Klishin's toe, which was superfluous to the laws of God and socialism, before Klishin went crazy and began killing the doctors, but they told him that if a sixth toe had grown on one foot, that was what the organism required, and no doctor would amputate a healthy toe, even if it was the ninth. For Klishin all this was the final straw and the weight of it finally drove him back in on himself; he carried around a time-bomb in his head, and under its crust of coal dust and soot his face became like the face of the colonel of the shadow forces, the way the faces of people burdened by a secret look alike. One gloomy autumn day Bedolagin arrived early at the boiler-room and ran into Klishin on the steps leading down to the basement. They went outside, and from the film of smoke clouding Klishin's eyes Bedolagin realized the bomb had exploded. Clutching a freshly sharpened chisel and lump-hammer in his fist, Klishin strode off in the direction of the hospital, taking the shortest route by the needle of the compass of revenge, which had been hovering in front of his eyes for a long, sleepless year. And he didn't utter a single word all the way from the school to the hospital, he walked into the hospital without saying a word, walked along the corridor between the benches outside the surgeon's office and walked into the office, still without saying a word, leaving the door open behind him. Without so much as a glance at the surgeon, the young nurse and the old man who was always laughing who'd stepped on a nail, he pulled up a wooden stool, took off his left boot, unwound his puttee, set his foot on the stool, set the sharpened edge of the chisel against the base of the sixth toe with a swift, precise movement, and before the surgeon could utter his

bloodcurdling scream, before the young nurse could go darting
out into the corridor, he took a short swing and struck the lump-
hammer hard against the haft of the chisel. Then he dropped the
tools and sank down slowly on to a stool, victorious in the war
he'd been waging with himself like an enemy since the absence of
an enemy had made him transform his post-war life into an
implacable, single-minded effort at self-destruction, still not
understanding the reasons for the sixth toe's appearance, but
vaguely sensing that he'd sharpened the chisel in order to slice
away the meaning of his life for the past year.

The severing of the sixth toe was the most outrageous and
scandalous event in the village that year, and even though the
old woman who lived at the edge of the village absolutely con-
demned what Klishin had done and thereby substantially
undermined her own authority, which she had believed was
indisputable, even though many women forbade their children
to go near Klishin so that he wouldn't advise them to cut out
their stomachs when there was nothing to eat, most people saw
his act as a triumph of the human spirit over physical pain, and
the old woman's warning that that way of viewing things would
inevitably lead to adulation of the self-mutilator and the suicide
was drowned in a deep sea of distrust, on the bottom of which
reposed plans for flights to the moon, the mathematical formu-
lae for splitting the atom and scientific materials on the nature of
genetic inheritance; in addition, a rumour began that in the distant city, where the colonel was leading the shadow forces in the
assault against the bearers of the idea of Caesar, the father of the
extra-uterine economy and personification of a Russia that had
washed itself and brushed its teeth had solemnly declared from
the tribune that the chisel and lump-hammer were the right
tools to use for settling accounts with objectionable toes on the
flat feet of the state debt.

Meanwhile the artist Pal, who started this rumour, stood in the market with his sparse, untrimmed light-brown hair straggling out from under his tattered, wide-brimmed brown hat, facing into a strident wind of human voices that buried beneath its swirling dust the silence of the neatly laid-out cobs of corn, socks, threads and phonograph needles, with the plywood board displaying his small, bright-coloured still-lifes of delicate spring flowers and picturesque drawings of genuflecting cavaliers and comely ladies in white ballgowns, and the reproachful glance of his moist, velvety eyes slid over the crowd and his pale, thin face, still the face of a fifteen-year-old boy ready to burst into tears at any moment, even though he was already thirty, was thrown upwards and back in mute reproach to his height of only one and a half metres, so that his smooth, pointed, hairless chin protruded like a cornice above the thin, white neck which disappeared into the raised collar of his long, motheaten coat with the skirts that almost dragged along the ground as he walked, lending a homeless, neglected and tearfully offended air to his thin, angular figure. He didn't hear the people who greeted him without any intention of buying his drawings, he heard but he didn't understand and he wouldn't have been able to repeat their words of invocation and shouts of indignation, which existed in his mind as the never-ending, continuous howling with which the wind sweeps away litter and sins in a world devoid of absolute silence, he didn't notice the dust raised by the wind settling on the sky-blue flowers of his still-lifes, so deeply engrossed was he in his own reflections, stepping cautiously through the shifting sands of commercial calculation, seeking a path leading to riches identical with the path of profligate spending, his gaze directed mutely over the bobbing, drifting, nodding heads. But at some particular moment which no one saw, all of this came to an end, his pale face was distorted by a grimace of fury and the next second the plywood sheet on which his drawings were displayed was sent crashing to the ground by a kick from a foot that flung apart the skirts of his coat. The trader on the left recoiled awkwardly and clumsily, expecting to see the gleam of the knife that invariably appeared in the artist's hand in his moments of uncontrollable rage, and a big woman with heavy breasts squatted down ponderously, spreading her massive knees, in order to pick up a drawing that had fallen at her feet, but the artist Pal said in a muffled hiss, 'Don't touch it,' and he said, 'Don't touch it, I said, you lousy bitch,' and then he said, 'You'll have time for that when I've gone, but don't touch it now.' Then the corners of his mouth curved down in self-pity, he flung his face up to the sky, and they watched him turn his back on them and go trudging off silently into the village, his thin legs getting tangled in the dusty, tattered skirts of his coat and his head still thrown back as though he was carrying a chalice containing his own heart on his forehead.

The artist Pal never said a word to anybody on that day, when after going down into the school boiler-room in order not to go on wandering endlessly, he spotted a source of wealth in Bedolagin and certain ideas were born in his head, and he never said a word to anybody for a very long time, even when those ideas had assumed firm substance as a result of certain calculations and checks that he made, partly in order to assure himself of his own artistic ability and partly to ensure that his efforts would not be wasted. He went to the next village, where there was a working church that had been damaged in the war and was being restored little by little by people who were deafened by the nocturnal howling of their consciences and were in desperate need of forgiveness and succour. But while the people had managed to block up the shell-holes with stones and bricks, shore up the slippage of the ground, fill in the nearby bomb craters and plaster the north wall with grey clay where it had been scarred by bullets, as well as tidy up the small hall and the vestibule, where they sold little crosses and icons the size of a matchbox for hanging round your neck, they weren't able to paint pictures of the faces of the saints which had been carried off, burnt or simply shot up by the soldiers of both armies. And so almost everything that makes a church a church on the inside was completely missing, and where it wasn't missing, it had been replaced by crude copies which, in the company of the few surviving icons with faces shot up by bullets, inspired alarm and trepidation in those who came in hopes of reconciliation with their own consciences and of finding God. And they would stop in the middle of the cold, painstakingly tidy hall of the church, where even the tiniest grains of dust preserved a ghostly vision of the deadly battle of many years ago, they would hear the firing and the shouting still echoing in the chime of the bells overhead and see the thick clumps of time lying undisturbed by any draught in the dark corners, preserving the very moment of killing, they would smell the dry odour of gunpowder and mouse droppings in the motionless air, and all of them were aware that every smell in a church has its own secret meaning which defines the meaning of existence itself, and they would pray, addressing their prayers to the one whose tall, white forehead had been pierced through, or to the one who observed them with one eye and a hole in place of the second. When the artist Pal, who had no skill in depicting human faces and no desire to depict them, for in his opinion they were not worth even a fraction of the effort involved, spotted in Bedolagin's face a certain ghastly, churchly resignation and all-forgiving meekness, and read in his eyes the sign of the inevitable disaster inherited by Bedolagin with the house, the shed for firewood and the cellar by the black apple tree, with the woman who had come to him just once and the dreams in which a pregnant cat clung to him with the sharp needles of its teeth sunk into his scrotum and, finally, with a face that attracted the lies and sins of the world like a magnet, then the artist offered his services to the church. Before setting a price, he made an arrangement with the church people for the supply of canvases and paint, and he also asked permission to borrow the surviving icon frames covered in cracked lacquer for a while, in order to mount his finished canvases in them himself, because he understood that no matter how well he might paint a canvas, it would always look better in an old frame than rolled up and then unrolled for inspection. Having received permission, he set a price that was neither low nor high, but more like a trial offer. Then he lugged the canvases, frames and paints back home and sat with his back to the window and the light, scribbling on sheets of paper for three days, first of all drawing on each sheet a yellow halo which, in his opinion, would lend an initial mysterious, sub-missive wisdom to the face that had existed beneath a halo since time immemorial and also counteract in advance the signs of imperfection and haste in his work. And when at the conclusion of the third day he survived his final creation and was satisfied, he did something he should not have done and never would have done, if he had been a historian or a politician; he painted out the halo, and when he looked for the first time at the face he had depicted when its golden halo was taken away, he felt the thick sap of fury flooding his brain and his hands seemed to be crumbling as they fumbled vainly for the knife. But afterwards, when the fit of rage had passed, he realized it was not important, and on the fourth day he showed up at the school boiler-room and told Klishin and Bedolagin just what he had in mind, prom-ising to give them half of the earnings to share between them. Then later, sitting in his room with his back to the window and the light, with an easel cobbled together out of crooked laths set in front of him, he said to Bedolagin: think about the things that you once had and lost, and Bedolagin thought about the grave of his hopes, entwined in the roots of the black apple tree as he stood over it at the threshold of autumn, after the time they'd suggested he should play the woman backside frontwards and prompted him to a murder that had never been committed, but before he'd rid himself of the smell of new-born life by replacing it with the smell of smoke and soot.

Then it grew dark, the artist Pal stopped working and Bedolagin went home. And as soon as his house came into sight among the other houses of the village, he saw a shadow through the wall and thought there must be someone inside. Almost convinced of his ability to see through walls, he went into the yard and up the steps of the porch, opened the door, went through the entrance hall that smelled of tarpaulin boots and then of mould, and over by the window in the room he saw Anna. He stood in the doorway without saying anything, invincibly dead, and his heavy, nerveless arms dangled idly downwards, drained of strength, of blood and the rigidity of their bones, like wet ropes, and she seemed even less real to him than the woman who had walked through desires and dreams across the withered wormwood that night, but now he didn't need her. And as soon as he realized she really had come back and it was her shadow he'd seen through the walls of the house as though he was looking through thin curtains against the light, and it really was her standing there now by the window, the same as ever, only thinner and pinched-looking, painfully beautiful, but ready as ever to conquer fortresses, shatter bastions with the power of her weakness, smash gates and break open locks, scorch his brains with the fragility of her thinness, ready to blow up the world in order to create everything anew from

the beginning and begin living over again, but wisely and without mistakes, he said, 'Get lost!' – sure in himself that he'd only
remember she'd come back until he fell asleep and by tomorrow
he'd forget, so he'd have to see her again in the morning and say
what he'd said today. But when he woke, he remembered quite
clearly that Anna had been in the house, he remembered in his
very first waking second, even before he noticed that she'd taken
off his boots and his work jacket that stank of smoke and soot.
She was sitting at the table watching him and when he got up
and put on his newly cleaned boots and jacket, she said in an
expressionless voice, 'Your friends came to see you,' and she
said, 'I know that artist, he's crazy,' and then she went on slowly,
ignoring his sullen silence, 'I told them scum like them have no
business round here.' He looked at her with a sullen, blank
expression, guessing she'd said this with something in mind,
she was obviously expecting an outburst of bitter fury, she'd
braced herself for curses and blows, and suddenly as he looked
at her pale, tense face and saw in her big, wide eyes the desire to
be punished, not for what she'd just said, but because she'd once
left him for another man, he thought he didn't need to raise his
hand to her, because her father's hand was already raised and
waiting for her to appear in order to beat the living breath out of
her.

But Anna's father didn't even get up from his log when
Bedolagin told him she'd turned up, he just sat there hunched
over, ferociously cracking large sunflower seeds with his teeth,
with his short bandy legs made for walking and not for gripping
the flanks of a horse tucked up under him, and he said coldly, 'So
what?' – and he said, 'So she's back,' and then he said calmly, 'So
smash her face in, say her father told you to.' Bedolagin turned
to leave, but Anna's father said, 'Stop,' and he said, 'Wait,' and
then he said, 'Let's go into the house and have a drop of vodka.'

They drank some vodka and some home brew coloured with a herb, and then Anna's father said, 'Give her a child,' and he said, 'Do it, I tell you.' Bedolagin said, 'Okay.' Anna's father knitted his thick, sun-bleached eyebrows and said, 'Do it.' Bedolagin said, 'Yes,' and he said, 'I will,' and he said, 'Definitely,' and then he said, 'One, two, three, four kids.' Anna's father said, 'What are you raving about?' Bedolagin said, 'Twenty, thirty, forty kids, a hundred kids, till she shouts out she's had enough.' Anna's father grinned and said, 'She won't shout out.' Bedolagin said, 'She will.' Anna's father said, 'She won't,' and he asked, 'Do you know why?' Bedolagin said, 'Why?' Anna's father said, 'She won't have any kids,' and he said, 'Not one.' Bedolagin asked, 'Why?' Anna's father said, 'Ask her,' and he said, 'She'll tell you.' Bedolagin said, 'Okay,' and he said, 'All right,' and then he said, 'D'you know why I came to see you?' Anna's father said, 'I know.' Bedolagin said, 'No you don't.' Anna's father said, 'Why?' Bedolagin stood up and said, 'So you'd go and kill her.' Then he left.

Then Anna took him in hand, casting aside affectation, stealthy approaches and sounding out the ground, she took him in hand, not gradually and imperceptibly, but straight away, as though any other way was impossible, as though she had gone away to the city by mutual agreement with him in order to come back at the appointed time, and that time had now arrived; without saying anything more than was necessary, without attempting to avoid saying anything that was necessary, she appeared in his house like the handmaiden of fate, she introduced a kind of ritual conversation over breakfast, lunch and supper when Bedolagin was at home, as though everything had been decided ages ago, already discussed and settled when they were still children, and there was nothing else left to say. She wrote a letter to the half-blind woman, inquiring after her health, and sent her a New Year card, signing it with Bedolagin's name and her own; she would not let Klishin and the artist Pal set foot inside the door, having identified them as a source of evil, and she told them to go to hell; she got herself a job at the local post office delivering letters and newspapers, and when her father said that the only reason she'd taken work as a post-woman was in order to intercept letters addressed to her by her fancy man in the city she told him to mind his own business. She assumed an indestructible patience and a stubbornness that made Klishin's stubbornness seem like the stubbornness of a fractious child who doesn't want to pee in the potty; mistaking the armour of death for an armour of ice, she armed herself with the likeness of a drill, intending to drill a way through to his heart at any cost, even if she had to break his ribs. And she was deceived, deceived by the taciturn, calm consent with which he shared his bed with her, the taciturn imperturbability with which he accepted anything that she said, by the voice in which he greeted her and took his leave of her, because too little time had gone by for her to understand and then believe that there was not and never had been any way to break through the absolute silence of his heart. And so she lived in the refusal to accept that times had changed, without trying to justify or whitewash herself, burying her past deeper than any dead man was ever buried, but not trying to make out that she was born yesterday, for she had to bring into operation the experience she had acquired of life. She made no secret of her intentions, she spoke boldly and menacingly, saying, 'Yes, I need a hus-band,' and she said, 'Just you try taking him away from me!' And the eyes in her delicate, beautiful face glittered as though she was already fighting against the entire world with a pitchfork caked with dung clutched in her thin, almost transparent hands.

The artist Pal painted three canvases in a very short period; he gave Bedolagin the shard of a mirror and Bedolagin looked into

the shard and then looked at the canvas and he saw a remark-
able, even depressing likeness; he remembered his own face,
which he'd only seen in a mirror once, immediately after the
war, when he was just barely fourteen, and then forgotten a long
time ago. The artist Pal knew the canvases were painted badly,
but he said they were painted better than the ones hanging in the
church. He took the canvases to the church one by one at inter-
vals of five days, and when the church people, extremely
amazed, asked how long he spent on a single canvas, he told
them he worked on the sketches for a year and painted the canvases using a slide-rule, which really confused them. Then he
began painting the fourth and final canvas of the commission,
but he never finished it, and Bedolagin was to blame because his
inability to control the dark power of his inheritance of poisoned blood, which dominated his brain, rendered him insane
during the hours he spent in a drunken stupor, inciting him to
actions with fatal consequences that he could have foreseen
when he was a child, but not now, when he was forbidden to
foresee and bidden to act. And three days after the artist Pal
sold the church the third canvas mounted in an old frame and
had begun working on the fourth, Bedolagin, drunk as a swine,
left the boiler-room and set out for the church in the neigh-
bouring village along the wide road eroded by the rains; unable
to feel his feet, he kept falling down and getting up again, feeling only the slow, smooth falling and the soft, slippery earth, and
his body, no longer able to feel pain, turned over, got up and
straightened itself again, obeying the same power that had led
every cell in the one-armed man's body to extinction and death.
And he walked into the church in broad daylight, dead-drunk in
his dirty, wet jacket and in squelching boots covered in liquid
mud. Barely dragging his feet along, he went through into the
hall of the church and stopped, steadying himself with his hand

against the wall, and looked at the artist Pal's canvases in the old frames with his dull, lifeless, unblinking eyes, recognizing himself, and it was only five minutes later, still not having blinked once, that he looked around, because he thought he heard a distant sound, gradually growing louder, and the noise died away and he saw people frozen in immobility. He looked at them without speaking and their lips moved as they silently pronounced words, but he could have shouted out loud, fallen into hysterics, created an uproar, and none of it would have had any effect, the silence would have swallowed it up before it could shape itself into living sound and no one would have noticed anything, because something they had noticed earlier had plunged the people into a salutary oblivion which alone was capable of saving their reason. And then Bedolagin slowly raised his hand with the index finger extended and the hand froze in mid-air when the finger was aligned with one of the icons and then the hand moved sideways, pointing to the two others and he said calmly, quietly but clearly, 'Take them down,' and still supporting himself against the wall, he repeated, 'Take them down,' and then, dragging his feet heavily, he left the church, but his hand remained hanging in the air in the church and it hung there until the icons he had pointed at were taken down.

He made his way home, falling and getting up again, along the same rain-eroded road, and without even looking at Anna he slumped on to the bed in his wet jacket and boots and slept for the rest of the day and all the night, but he woke up without his jacket and without his boots. He put on his still damp but clean boots and went to the doorway.

Anna was standing in the middle of the yard, she'd put down the battered old German jerry-can filled with kerosene and was holding a stick in her thin, almost transparent hand, and her eyes were blazing in despairing anger, and from the doorway

Bedolagin heard her shout, 'Clear off out of here, you damn bastards, clear off,' and he saw them standing by the wicket-gate in
the fence, already inside the yard, he saw the artist Pal pull the
knife out of the pocket of his long, narrow coat with that movement the whole village knew, as impossible to catch as the
parting of the ends of a tautly stretched cable, when Anna raised
the stick over her head and went for them, obviously having
decided either to die or to take a rest from everything in a hospital bed with a gash torn in the belly she no longer cared for
since she'd found out she couldn't have children. And then the
artist Pal was faced with the necessity of killing someone, but he
quickly mastered the confusion caused by his disbelief that
anyone would risk going for him when he had his knife, because
he realized that murder had been committed in precisely this way
and no other ever since life was first conceived, and he realized
that once he'd adopted the habit of pulling his knife out of his
pocket at the first thing anyone said wrong, in the vain attempt
to make himself taller than he was, then sooner or later he would
have to make use of it. Anna saw all of this, she understood all of
it from his eyes and she stopped for a second, then carried on
towards him; and there was something she wanted to say, but she
couldn't, she was filled with despair and curiosity, like before the
first time she was physically intimate with a man, the only time,
so long ago, when it had ever really meant anything. And then
Bedolagin went dashing towards them from the porch, his mouth
open wide in a soundless cry, and he stumbled and fell full-
stretch in the middle of the yard. Then Klishin stepped towards
Anna and she took a swing at him, but he took the blow on his
arm, grabbed the stick out of her hand and threw it aside. Then
he slowly turned to face the artist Pal, who was waiting for Anna,
every now and then adjusting the grip of his thin fingers on the
handle of the knife, screwed up one eye and said in a low, calm

voice, 'Have you really decided to do for her?' And after a pause he asked again, softly, 'Have you?' Pal said in a low hiss, 'Yes, I have,' and he said, 'I won't let any fucking bitch yell at me,' and then he said, 'Keep out of it.' He looked obstinately into Klishin's face and saw what had always been hidden under the crust of dust and soot, what he saw was not a face but a landslide of black stones frozen in mid-flight, halted and frozen by force of will, he saw a man whom nothing could please or displease, irritate or leave indifferent, aggrieve or gladden, he saw a man capable only of loving or hating without exception, a spirit woven out of only two feelings and not hundreds, a life consisting entirely of mute love and mute hatred, all of a piece but quite goalless, unrelenting in the face of obstacles, created in extremity and nourished on extremity. And in his stupor he allowed Klishin's tough fingers to tear the knife from his hand, his heart was confused and he couldn't stir a muscle, and finally, when he regained the power of movement, he tried to hit Klishin, but he couldn't even reach his face, and then he threw himself on him in a fury, but that was just like beating on cast-iron gates with a straw, and when Klishin's fist crunched into his head, it was as though an aeroplane flying by had clipped him with its wing. Pal had anticipated this moment and had time to think it was better this way than throwing himself on Klishin over and over again without the slightest hope. And then without saying a word Klishin bent down, picked up the artist Pal, slung him across his shoulder and carried him all the way through the village without even limping, walking as freely and surely as the time he walked to the hospital to cut off his sixth toe, and he didn't put the artist Pal down until he was in his house, in the corner of the room with the easel cobbled together out of crooked laths and Bedolagin's unfinished face on the canvas that there was no need to finish any more, because it was impossible to sell.

At the end of November Anna's period failed to arrive. For the next two weeks she went round the house doing all the things she always did, as though nothing had happened. She told herself: I haven't changed, and she told herself: Nothing's changed. She asked herself: Why did they tell me it was impossible? She asked herself: How could he, who can't do anything, do what no one else could do? And then she said: Who knows why I might have lost them? – seeking the reasons for her mysterious non-conception, superstitiously driving away hope, as though its very appearance threatened hopelessness and lack of faith in the earth. And the two weeks went by as though she was deep under water that blunted the former rapidity of her movements but endowed her with the hearing of a bat, only not so she could save herself, but so she could hear the rustling of life even in the falling of a leaf.

She sat on the bed, and though she was firmly convinced of the opposite, she told herself: It can't have happened, watching as Bedolagin put on his work jacket and his boots and then looked at her calmly with his hands in his pockets and said, 'I won't be back today,' said what he always said if she was within hearing of his voice and perhaps even when she couldn't hear him, then turned and went out. She watched him go, knowing already for certain that today she would dream about him; she sat there, not noticing how long the night was, her thin hands folded on her knees, she put out the light and thought in the twilight silence, then two hours before dawn she lay down without getting undressed and fell asleep the moment she closed her eyes.

Suddenly, out of nowhere, he was there, walking along in his dirty jacket and heavy boots, treading silently over the ground, lifeless, not flesh and blood, gathering into himself the dark void of the night like the dressed skin of a slaughtered beast, not answering to anyone or anything because he'd annihilated every feeling inside himself, including even his animal instincts, he walked along the common and fell into a pile of leaves neatly gathered together by the children before they set light to it, and her dream was saturated with the scent of autumn, filled with the loud rustling of dry leaves as he burrowed into them, burying himself completely in order to stop dead still the moment his fingers touched the ground. But they were already running on their way – small, dark, skinny and just – running to set fire to the leaves they had been collecting all autumn long, from the beginning of September to the beginning of December, and flames were flaring up in their hands.

Anna woke up and went running out of the house without her shoes and she ran through the village in the darkness of the new day with her bare feet scarcely touching the cold, frozen ground, and when the school building finally came into sight, with the garden to the right of it, she saw the white leaf-smoke drifting slowly up into the sky above the black trees. Then she stopped and stood gazing at the white smoke, and then she said, 'O God,' and she said, 'O God,' and then she said, 'Save him.'

# Hare's Eye*

I hated that kid.

It was just my luck to serve in the army with him.

Every day I saw that skinny, gangling body shrouded in a uniform that was so big for him he could take it off without unfastening the buttons, those heavy boots bent out of shape by his crooked feet, with no steel tips on the worn-down heels; those shoulders, as narrow as the blade of an oar; that face, about as lovely as a blob of solidified magma – I'd have liked to take a look at the woman who had him and find out what month disaster struck, but Bragin said only very gifted people can be so ugly and morbidly delicate. And then he said, 'Just look, his

* Hare's eye or lagophtalmos: a disease of the eye preventing complete closure of the eyelids.

head's too heavy for his neck, look, it's flopped over sideways like a two-month-old baby's.' And Nun, who used to clean out the cages in a zoo, said, 'A wolf pack always kills off a wolf that's weak or sick, because when it comes down to it the strong and healthy wolves can't afford to let him live.'

I hated that kid even before I knew he used to be a pianist and his name was Vensky.

Vensky was sent to us from a radio operators' training unit. He turned up at company base an hour before evening roll-call one boring evening, dropped his kitbag and bunched-up greatcoat on the floor in the middle of the passage between the two-tier bunks and stood there without saying a word, gazing around in dismay as though he'd fallen into a deep hole and didn't know how to clamber out. He ran that worried, frightened gaze over everyone until finally he lit on me. For a few seconds we looked into each other's eyes. My muscles involuntarily tensed up. I froze, as though I was getting ready to dodge a knife. He smiled and relaxed.

Vensky started behaving like someone who's about to ask you to lend him some money.

I developed this subconscious urge to keep as far away from him as possible. I didn't know why the hell he stuck so close to me – they don't like that sort of thing in the army – maybe he could sense something, maybe he'd seen something in a dream and his attempts to stick by my side were like a blind man's attempts to find a firm footing.

He always wandered about apart from the other soldiers – the air made farting noises in his boots – his face was twisted out of shape and his forehead wrinkled up under the pressure of some dull, hypochondriacal pain: he was nursing along a requiem for one of us, some combination of pain and music.

I was haunted by his face. Later on I realized I was appealing to that face on the nights when I didn't want to go on living.

He was always there beside me, smiling guiltily and wanting to talk.

I used to say to him, 'Listen you, get your ugly mug away from me.' He just stood there and smiled guiltily, like a child about to take away your toy.

I couldn't bear having to look at him all the time when the very sight of him made me want to make a run for it.

I used to say to him, 'Get your ugly bastard mug away from me.'

But I was wasting my breath. He'd chosen me.

I changed a lot. People were afraid of me, the way they're afraid of the dark and of open graves. I was so charged up with fury I could have blown up bridges. I became dangerous – some brainless, dumb-animal fear of man was resurrected inside me – I was always on my guard, saw danger everywhere. I faced my enemy with blind fury and the longer it went on, the more I realized my enemy would live as long as I was alive, the only way he'd die was in me, together with me, but not outside me.

I thought I could detect the stubborn, implacable precision of a compass in the actions of this scrawny little runt. His life was ruled by an infallible intuition that made his feet tread where the ground would never gape open underneath him and carry his body safely past a thousand deaths and drunken lives; made him close his eyes where other people are blinded, leave a spot where anyone else would have been crushed by a falling tree; the precise, unfailing calculation of an ancient instinct confirming a man's absolute, morbid belief in the supreme importance of his own life and his power to do great things. Raised in purity and innocence, he was afraid of blood, puked at the sight of someone else's puke, didn't like stray dogs but had a boundless love for his mother, that prudent human bitch who'd protected and taught him.

In spring they put Vensky in the medical unit.

The windows of the medical unit overlooked the yard of our barracks. No matter what time it was when I walked past, there was Vensky's head hovering behind the cross of the window-frame. He would look out at me, clutching the window-sill, twisting his yellow face into a worried smile. He looked really bad. I could hardly resist the urge to dance.

Out of malicious curiosity I used to go to the clinic and try to read Vensky's medical notes, but I couldn't make out a damn thing apart from the fact that he was ill – if they taught a monkey to write by clutching the pen between its feet, its writing would be easier to read and understand than any doctor's.

After two weeks Vensky was discharged.

He came into the mess hall and sat down at the same table as me. I was slowly eating my pearl barley, contemplating my dirty hands. From somewhere Vensky produced half a stick of smoked salami, sliced it with a blunt penknife and handed it out to everyone sitting at our table.

'Damn you. You're back again,' I growled angrily. 'Damn you, you filthy whore.'

I reached out for the bread. Vensky quickly leaned across the table and put a piece of bread with a slice of salami beside my plate. I looked at the bread plate for a few seconds, feeling the thick fumes of rage swirling in my brain, then I slammed my fist down on the table and swept his stinking salami and my plate on to the floor. Everybody went quiet. There weren't any officers in the mess. I got up and went out.

The sunlight streamed down from the sky like golden sand.

I wanted to be alone.

I wanted to be alone like I was five years earlier, when I was lying beside the sea: it started raining, everybody collected up their stuff and left, leaving me there on the wet gravel, watching the wind lift small, salty bursts of spray off the sea, stretch the little waterspout out into a slim female figure and waltz it across the waves.

But nobody's about to leave this place, not even if it starts raining bones.

That night I couldn't get to sleep for a long time, I was delirious, there were ghostly white spots – human faces – drifting in front of my eyes. The number of faces gradually increased and they kept moving faster – millions of human faces, immortalized for their heroism and ignominy, debauchery and war by the historians, those impartial peddlers of lies. They were suffering from cold, hunger, malaria, poverty, indigence, inadequacy, drunkenness, but they gave thanks to God – they tried not to stand out too much, not to set themselves up for a fall, not to make war, not to die – they were sick, healthy, illegitimate, mad – they wanted just to slip past under the sun quietly and inconspicuously, have children quietly and inconspicuously – a crowd of millions moving without a sound. From time to time one of them broke away and cried out, 'Stop, that's not the way,' and he was killed, crushed under a stone slab of envy, poisoned by a horse's dose of brucine, riddled with bullets; disappeared without trace when he went into the forest to pay his respects to fate.

Everything comes to an end when I'm ready to begin.

I came to, then fell asleep, and the gigantic wall of faces crumbled.

At five in the morning I woke up completely and lay without moving, listening to the snuffling and snoring and the creaking of rusty bedsprings under slumbering bodies. Then I got up, put on my boots, grabbed my cigarettes and went to the washroom. I smoked, inhaling deeply and looking out of the window. There was a strong smell of Lysol solution and dirty underclothes.

Someone came into the washroom. I looked round and saw Vensky. He was wearing large, crumpled black shorts and one of the torn vests that often came with the deliveries of clean underclothes from the divisional laundry. He smiled guiltily, everything about him expressing commiseration.

The whites of his eyes were as yellow as uncleaned teeth.

He took a few steps towards me.

I put my cigarette on the windowsill.

He twisted his face up, preparing to say something. But I couldn't give a damn whatever he might say. Now I had the chance to do at least the little that could be done. I waited until he got close and then without taking a swing I hit him sharp and clean. His head jerked to one side, his legs buckled and he fell. I screwed up my eyes and watched as he got up; I waited to see what he'd say, I felt every blow I struck would be a relief to him after fate decided to release us from each other. He'd known that sooner or later I'd give him a beating, but he'd been looking for a chance to see me alone – that meant he'd wanted this to happen. And apart from that, he wanted to explain something.

He got up and said, 'There's no point in that.'

It seems he was absolutely sure he had to be with me no matter what and put up with all my outbursts.

I ought to have run for it, but I hit him again. He fell and couldn't get up for a long time. There was blood coming out of his mouth.

He said, 'There's no point in that.'

The next day I was given seven days in the lock-up.

Vensky went to the company commander and said he started the fight, so if they jailed anyone they should jail us both, but the commander knew me inside out and he wouldn't listen to him; then Vensky insulted a sergeant and they gave him three days. He was certain he just had to be with me everywhere. But before we could serve the time both of us had to have a medical. At the medical unit they refused to allow Vensky to be jailed.

Two days later I was shipped off to the garrison guardhouse.

The guards took my money and documents, everything with a sharp edge and everything I could hang myself with; they searched me for cigarettes, going through my pockets, sticking their fingers under my shoulder-straps, shaking out my boots after they took out the insoles, feeling along the seams of my clothes. Then they drew up a list of what they'd taken from me, gave it to me to sign, led me to my cell, took the lock off the fold-down bunk and told me I could sleep till tomorrow, because today wouldn't count as part of my time and they wouldn't be feeding me today.

It was a four-man cell – a door covered with sheet iron and painted green, with a spyhole at eye level, grey concrete walls, and in the wall opposite the door a crudely broken through air vent leading out into the yard, in the corner a forty-litre tank of drinking water and a mug. Nothing else.

I collapsed on the wooden bunk and fell asleep. I was woken by the heavy tramping of boots along the corridor. It was late. The prisoners were back from the work site. At lights out I discovered there were two others in the cell with me – a swarthy marine and a tall, fat Uzbek; they came into the cell, gave me a surly glance and slumped on to their bunks. The guards locked the door from the outside and the cat's eye of the dim two-twenty-volt duty lamp lit up inside the cell.

The marine was mumbling and muttering about how he hadn't had time to go and relieve himself and now he'd have to wait till morning, because they didn't let you out of the cells at night. The Uzbek said nothing, pretending not to understand Russian. They were both in for ten days for going absent without leave – the marine said he'd run off to see a woman, but no one knew where the Uzbek had gone. The marine had already done two days and the Uzbek had done three.

At night the cell was cold and damp.

They got the guardhouse up at five in the morning.

We lined up in the corridor and waited sullenly to be detailed off.

They divided us into groups of ten to fifteen men, led us outside, gave out spades, crowbars and litters for shifting rubble, and told us who was working where. Our group was herded off to an abandoned piece of wasteland a long way away to dig ditches, either for garbage or for food waste. We were followed by two guards with machine-guns. One of them, a lanky, melancholy young guy, sat off to one side on an upturned rusty bucket, resting his machine-gun on his knees with the barrel pointing in our direction and lazily sculpting toys out of scrap rubber.

It was a long time since I'd run that far, and I'd never run that far with a litter and a crowbar.

By lunchtime the Uzbek was half-dead, and from lunch to suppertime he just fiddled feebly with his spade and cried into the hole he'd dug.

We were as dirty as branches dragged out of a bog.

At night I had cramps in my legs.

The marine's snoring was like someone dragging a three metre-long chest of drawers across concrete.

I soon got used to the routine and ran through everything automatically, hardly even getting tired. But the Uzbek couldn't get used to it and he cried every day.

On the sixth day the marine, lying stretched out on his bunk, said, 'You're off tomorrow. And the next day it's my turn.' He grinned, looking at the Uzbek: 'It's not so bad in here, eh?' And he laughed.

The Uzbek began trembling in fury.

The marine said, 'The main thing is, the time passes quickly in here and the food's good.'

When it was almost morning I opened my eyes and saw the Uzbek sitting on his bunk, swaying from side to side with his hands pressed between his knees. Then he got up and walked across the cell, looking to see whether the marine was asleep, sat back down again and looked carefully across at me. I didn't budge. Then he went over to the tank of drinking water and took off the lid. I raised my head. The Uzbek was unfastening his trousers. I stood up. He swung round to face me. The dull light of the lamp was reflected in his staring black eyes.

I snarled at him: 'Why, you filthy pig!'

His face twisted into a grimace and he came at me. I stood my ground and thought, if he throws a hook my number's up, but he threw a straight right, I dodged to the left, but not quickly enough and his fist caught my neck, almost taking half my head off. Inertia kept the Uzbek coming towards me and I kneed him in the groin. He grunted, showering out spit, and doubled over. I took a step backwards and hammered at him with my fists until he slumped on to the floor. The marine was sitting on his bunk rubbing his eyes. I told him what it was all about and we lifted up the Uzbek and helped him across to his bunk. Gasping for breath, he said to me, 'Bastard. Bastard. Tomorrow I tell. You stay ten days more here. Bastard. Stay here . . . Ten days more.'

The marine whispered insistently to the Uzbek, 'He'll get five days at most for the fight, but for pissing in the drinking water you'll get at least ten.' The Uzbek, still gasping for breath, whispered, 'I not piss.' But the marine whispered, 'Who knows that? They're not going to test it, we'll tell the same story and they'll believe us.' The Uzbek said nothing, breathing heavily, and then he whispered, 'But what I say? Why face like this, eh?' And the marine whispered, 'You'll tell them you banged your face against the wall in your sleep.' The Uzbek understood everything but he whispered, 'Not understand.' The marine lost patience and he whispered, 'What nationality are you?' The Uzbek whispered, 'Asphalt layer.'

The marine might as well not have bothered. Nobody asked any questions. In the morning the Uzbek was taken off back to his unit. Before he left he came over to me, put his arms round me and said, 'Dumb, dumb, understand,' and whispered, 'No, no.' Then he ran off.

They lined the rest of us up for work detail.

That day I got an extra five days for a fag-end under my bunk. I didn't know whether the Uzbek had tossed it under there or the guards had just been smoking in the cell.

The next day the marine got out.

I was left on my own. During the day I worked myself senseless. At nights I thought about Vensky.

Then my time was up.

They shipped me back to the unit.

I wanted to sleep more than I wanted to live.

It was wonderful weather. A golden web of sunlight strung out above the roofs of the buildings had snared all the birds over the town. There were people walking along the streets who would never meet Vensky.

There was no one at the company base. They'd all been taken off to the firing range to cut turf for camouflaging bunkers.

I sat down on my bunk and tried to take off the boots I hadn't taken off for twelve days, but I got nowhere. I got a bayonet from the duty sentry, slit the tops of the boots almost down to the soles, tossed the boots under the bunk, put on someone's tattered old slippers and hobbled off to see the master sergeant. I bought two packs of cigarettes from him, took a magazine, grabbed a stool and went off to the washroom. I sat by the

window, smoking and reading. I read a story about a little country girl and a huge pig, then I read some poems printed under a
photograph of a beautiful young woman. The poems were no
good, but the woman was so beautiful only someone who could-
n't get it up could have refused to publish her poems. Then I
looked through the strip cartoons.

Someone touched me on the shoulder. I looked up and saw
Vensky.

He smiled his martyr's smile and said, 'I didn't tell anyone
about the fight.'

I said, 'You go to hell.'

He blushed pink as a dog's tongue and said, 'I didn't say anything to anyone,' then he turned round and left. I think he was
crying. I'd be damned if he hadn't been suffering – all the time
he'd been thinking he was the one who'd done me wrong.

On Thursday the company commander fell in the company
and said there was a hundred-kilometre march over mountain
roads set for seven days' time. For the driver-mechanics that
meant seven days solid stuck under their armoured personnel
carriers. He read out the members of the teams. My radio operator was Nun. Vensky was radio operator in the team for
personnel carrier number 204, which made its place in the
column of march just ahead of mine, number 205. Their driver-
mechanic was Bragin.

They took us to the motor-vehicle depot.

Any other time I wouldn't have raised a finger, just hung
around the service zone or got some sleep in the storeroom. But
my presentiment of disaster was growing stronger.

I changed the oil in the motor, replaced the fuel pump, put in
a new starter, checked the generator and the regulator and
changed the fuel filters, even though a lot of the others didn't
bother to use them. Anyone walking by must have thought I'd

gone crazy. I balanced the clutch, gave the steering and the entire braking system a thorough check. Then I remembered that on the last march the front left wheel boss had been overheating. I removed the wheel and the boss, changed the bearing and gave it a thick coat of grease. I was putting the wheel back, twisting the heavy assembly into place, when something made me look round and I saw Vensky standing about twenty paces away beside a big black can of Negrol, following every movement I made.

I realized everything I'd been doing was a waste of time and I squatted down on my haunches, staring stupidly at my dirty hands and the spanners under the wheel. And I felt like it was the end of a war, when you've no strength left to carry on living by hate and no willpower left to carry on living by nostalgia.

On Saturday they gave Nun a pass for a day's leave. He got the address of some sure-fire brunette from Bragin, took a wash and cleaned his teeth, ironed his uniform, got dressed and took off into town.

He came back on Sunday evening, glowing bright as a wandering comet, hardly made it through evening roll-call, got undressed, straightened his back which was scratched all over, from top to bottom, and set off at a leisurely pace to the washroom, angling his head so everyone could see the long, purple love-bite under his left ear.

For the next two days and nights he jabbered away without stopping. On the third day someone saw him walk listlessly out of the toilet, go over to his locker without saying a word, take out a clean sheet of paper, an envelope and some boot polish, put the paper on the floor, put on his boot and stand on the paper with the full length of his foot. Then he folded up the paper with the imprint of his boot sole, put it in an envelope, wrote the brunette's address on it and dropped the envelope in the company letterbox.

After lunch he came up to me with a distant, mournful look in his blue eyes, looked up as though he was expecting rain and said, 'Seems I've been dropped in it.'

I lit up, looked at Vensky, who was hanging about nearby with that damned guilty smile, and growled, 'I got dropped in it too, when I was born.'

Nun said, 'I've got to get to hospital.'

I asked him, 'What for?'

Nun said, 'To get myself checked out.' He paused and then he said, 'I went to the company commander . . . Told him I was feeling bad, like, had to get to hospital. Said he could find a replacement for the march.'

I asked, 'So what did he say?'

Nun said, 'He said okay, so Vensky can replace you.'

I waited for a moment, then said, 'You can go to hospital straight after the march.'

He stared at me and asked, 'Why?'

I said, 'Because you're my radio operator. That's good enough.'

Then I went to the medical unit. The medical instructor and I spent an hour and a half rummaging through all the drawers and first-aid kits and we found Vibramycin, Diazoline and Nistatin. I took the tablets and gave them to Nun.

On the twenty-fourth of April they sounded the alarm to get the company out of bed.

The column of armoured personnel carriers moved out of the company base, looped around the town, crossed the plateau and headed for the foothills.

The road was narrow and winding.

It was uphill and downhill by turns.

As I drove the personnel carrier I listened to how the engine was running.

I spat over my shoulder.

And then on one of the uphill stretches the carrier's motor died. I switched off the ignition, switched it back on again and tried using the starter-motor to turn the engine, but the starter was just idling.

In his misery Nun said, 'Something's burned out.'

I told him to shut his face. Then I climbed out on to the armour plating.

The two personnel carriers behind us had stopped and the rest were catching up with them. Bragin's carrier, the one in front, had stopped too. The first four were already out of view round a bend.

The company commander yelled through a megaphone from number 208. 'What's going on up there?' he yelled. 'Well?'

I could see the road was too narrow for them to get past us.

The pressure of the roaring engines on my eardrums was like being under ten metres of water.

'Tow them!' the company commander roared through his megaphone. 'Bragin, give them a tow,' he roared at Bragin, and he roared at me, 'Unfasten your towbar!'

I jumped down on to the ground and unfastened the towbar. Bragin backed up. I hooked on the towbar and climbed back into the carrier. Bragin set off with a sudden jerk. I saw the blue exhaust fumes through the triplex windscreen, I heard the towbar snap, and Bragin's carrier went roaring off uphill. Vensky, sitting on the armour plating of 204, leaned down to the hatch and told Bragin the towbar had broken off. Bragin braked and began slowly backing up. Cursing the world and its mother, I climbed out again, but Vensky had beaten me to it. His boots were covered in white dust. He was holding another towbar.

He said, 'It's okay, I'll hook it on.'

I stood aside, watching the pianist's deft, dexterous hands clumsily attach the towbar to the shackle, and felt like laughing out of spite. Finally he managed to hook the towbar to Bragin's carrier, turned his back to it and began attaching the other end to my shackle. It was only from the shadow creeping up Vensky's boot that I realized Bragin's carrier was rolling backwards – it often happens, you just sit there at the steering-wheel and start thinking about God knows what and your attention wanders.

Vensky was standing with his back to Bragin's carrier and trying to attach the towbar.

I saw the shadow on Vensky's back and realized that in two seconds he'd be crushed between the armoured personnel carriers.

Things always work themselves out; the more you talk about them, the longer it takes for anything to get done about them.

I didn't want to think and I didn't want to shout, because when it's curtains time, thinking and shouting are just plain stupid.

I jumped at the moment when Vensky raised his head, and when the rear wall of Bragin's transporter was only centimetres away from his back. I put all my life into that punch, everything that had been and everything that should have been. And before my bones crunched between the steel walls I saw Vensky's scraggy face as my punch tossed him into the air and he tumbled over like an unbreakable puppet and landed two metres away from the personnel carriers.

They laid me in the warm, soft dust at the edge of the road. Someone took off my helmet and stroked my hair. Probably Vensky.

I tell you, stop all this useless fucking about.

I tell you, there's no need to take me anywhere. Moving on makes sense for you. What makes sense for me is staying put.

But you don't hear me.

I don't open my eyes because I know what I'll see – the entire column has come to a halt, apart from the first four personnel carriers that went on out of sight round the bend.

I don't know if I'll be able to open my eyes. I can't feel anything inside myself. I can't separate your voices from the rumbling of falling stones and the rumbling of the firing range. I can't separate what's living from what's dead.

There's no need to take me anywhere.

. . . It's been on its way for a long time now, treading the grey roads lightly, silently, like ash settling.

Don't touch me.

I want to see this.

# The Root and the Goal

In the village they saw Baskakov begin building the house in early spring, after the foundations had been laid; through the low, rickety fence they saw him working away from dawn till dusk without lifting his head or taking any breaks for a bite to eat or a smoke, but no one ever saw him hurry. He slept just two metres away from the large, dilapidated dog-kennel, on a few planks nailed together, with his head resting on a pile of used rags, hardly bothering to undress, and wrapping himself in a piece of oiled tarpaulin that was drenched in dew by the morning. Nearby, slightly to one side of the kennel and the tub of water, lay a large grey dog of indeterminate breed, but from the colour and thickness of the fur on his withers, from his wild ululating ferocity and his sinewy backside, they could tell easily enough that the bitch who gave birth to him had kept company with a wolf-pack. The dog loved the rain and in spring he was always as dirty as a swamp buffalo. His chain was so long that he could patrol the entire yard, even its furthest corner; he slept during the day while his master was working, and at night lay beside him on the moonlit ground without making a sound, watching the gate with sinister eyes as translucent as mica, ready to pounce at the first creak of the hinges in the rabid fury of his half-and-half existence. In the morning Baskakov woke up, threw off the groundsheet, took a wash, fed the dog, ate something himself, and then worked unstintingly without a break until evening, chewing on oil-cake and never lifting his head even when he was building the roof, and through the low, rickety fence they saw him standing stooped over in the middle of the yard, pulverizing the air and the light with rapid, regular strokes of an axe, planing, sawing and hammering, as stubborn, hostile and mute as a nail half hammered home, paying no attention to anyone or anything around him.

He was supplied with bricks, cement and other building materials by his older brother, who was the chief engineer at the brick factory, and so in the village they were scarcely surprised, and even then it was mostly out of deep-rooted habit, at the sight of good-quality bricks actually being delivered on time. If they had known that the older brother was charging the younger brother twenty per cent over and above the state price for the bricks, ready to justify this by the fact that he was providing them on credit to a former convict, they would have stopped being surprised at all. The older brother put in an appearance every time the truck came with bricks and he watched in cold silence as the three men from the factory, who had come at his request or on his orders, sweated and strained to unload the bricks and his younger brother piled them up in wide, low stacks; he stood coldly aside, thickset and overweight for his height, his appearance a total contrast with his brother's, with a flabby, yellow face on which the lenses of his spectacles, perched above a flattened nose as broad as a boot heel, glinted in the light. When the unloading was over the older brother took out a sheet of paper and a pencil and the younger brother sat down on the bricks and wrote out promissory notes and the older brother coldly stuck them into his jacket pocket and left the yard without speaking, and the truck followed him out, its sides rattling in reply to the frenzied barking of the dog, which was set on a short chain. Only once did they exchange a brief word; the men unloading the bricks heard the older brother say contemptuously, 'Shut that bloody hound up, can't you?' And then for just a moment the younger brother opened the sluice gates of his soul that held back the seething force of whirlpools of cold, pure hatred, and told him through clenched teeth, 'That's what I keep him here for, to bark when vermin comes crawling into the yard.'

At the beginning of December the first snow fell and he went away, leaving the house unfinished; early one morning he tidied up the fenced-in yard, gathered his tools together and packed them away in a shed he had knocked together in a hurry, wired the gate shut and set off through the village at a steady, unhurried pace, one hand clutching his strapless rucksack tied shut with string and the other holding a two-metre leather lead stretched taut by the grey dog, with a dull snap-hook attached to its broad, rough collar jangling at its far end. He walked to the station, although there was a bus that went there every morning, a clanking iron box with broken windows replaced here and there by plywood, that teetered along on half-flat tyres with treads as bald as hen's eggs. When he walked past the shop where the bus was standing, the crowd of villagers parted to let him through, since they were sure he wouldn't alter his line of progress merely to oblige a small group of other people, because there was some incomprehensible force in him that made him move along the invisible rails of fate with an icy but unostentatious contempt quite different from the way they themselves moved; and as he silently walked between them, they caught the scent of a savage dampness on the wind.

At noon that same day the tools he had hidden in the shed were extracted and carried off on a truck by two men from the brick factory.

The unfinished house stood covered in snow all winter like some exclusion zone or baneful sacred mountain, and every inhabitant of the village, jealously cherishing the taboo, guarded the unfinished house against the least encroachment, not allowing children to play in it or tramps to stay there overnight. There was only one time that winter when the cold brick walls of the unfinished house provided shelter for a frail old hobo, whose long grey hair was crawling with insects and whose clothes stood stiff and erect like a stake, because there was less fabric in them than there was cement dust, vomit and excrement, moistened in his wanderings during the warm season, and now transformed by the frost into an icy armoured shell from which escape was no longer possible without resorting to a saw or a hot fire. But no sooner had he laid face down and covered his head with his thin, trembling hands in order to stop the wind howling in his ears and protect his face from the powdery snow flying in through the empty window-frames and the gaping arches where the doors would be, than the inhabitants of the village, acting on information from some urchin, armed themselves with sharpened spades, pitchforks and chains and advanced on the unfinished house, driven by a strange, incomprehensible sense of duty which charged their entire beings with the insistent droning of an incandescent electric coil. However, as soon as they came close to the rickety fence, the people in the front rows pulled up sharply, not daring to overstep the boundary line of the taboo that blazed brightly in their minds, and all they did was whoop and yell, waving their arms about in scattered bursts of shouting. And when the frail hobo crept out through the door opening, moving clumsily in the rigid clothing that was like a concrete pipe cast around the trunk of his body, still not properly awake, his watery eyes still half-hidden behind pale eyelids as thin as a placenta, and his ears still stopped up by the wind, they all suddenly fell silent and stood rooted to the spot, as though a flame had suddenly been turned to stone and all its numerous sparks had been turned to stone where they hung in the air when time itself was also turned to stone. And then one of them yelled out in a loud voice, 'There he is! There he is, the bloody so-and-so!' And immediately the sounds of their voices showered down on the hobo, together with the stones and lumps of ice they had managed to chip out of the frozen earth with the toes of their boots and shoes; and then he struggled to his feet, still snared in the nets of fatigue and somnolence, and lumbered off, swaying uncertainly, in the direction of the swamp, towards the tall dark willow trees, pursued by piercing cries and the whistling of ice.

Baskakov came back in March the next year. The first to see him was the blind boy who usually rose an hour before dawn, sensing the approach of morning with his skin, and sat by the window, leaning on the windowsill cluttered with matchboxes, constructing toy churches out of matches by touch. He saw him on the day before the March holiday, trudging through the spring mud at six o'clock in the morning with the tops of his phosphorescing boots turned down or cut off almost down to his ankles; in one hand he was holding the rucksack with no straps and in the other the leather lead, stretched taut by the grey dog. The boy dropped his matches, and feeling a burning pain deep inside his unseeing eyes, stared silently, fixedly, greedily over the dome of the unfinished matchstick church at the man's black, unbending back, at the black, indomitable back of his head that was like a heavy bell, and he went on looking until the man and the dog had dissolved into the familiar darkness of his two-year-old blindness.

At six o'clock in the morning on the seventh of March he ripped the wire off the gate, put the dog on the long, rusty chain and stood for a while beside the dog kennel, like a crumbling black mushroom gnawed hollow by burrowing ants, and then, without changing his clothes, without looking around or checking anything, he got down to work, setting about sweeping out of the house the wet trash and garbage that the winds had blown in during the winter. That summer he didn't work alone. Every day he was helped by several men from the brick factory, and almost every day his older brother turned up with scraps of paper and the stub of a pencil, staying just long enough to get the usual promissory note, himself determining the cost of building materials and labour that had cost him nothing, because most of the help with building the house was provided by soldiers convicted of theft who were eager to settle matters amicably, and furthermore the senior engineer, who was also the chairman of the local trade union committee, had fixed things so that the foremen entered their work days in the time book and they were paid by the factory at the same rate as men who sorted bricks; but while the older brother didn't charge the younger a high rate for labour, apparently conforming the amounts in the promissory notes to the average factory pay for a brick-sorter, for the building materials – and in the village they suspected the materials hadn't cost him anything, either – he charged an exorbitant price, no doubt applying a system of compensatory tariffs in the manner of those traders who wanted to establish a compensatory tariff for cottage cheese made from milk from a cow raised on a private farm such that the cost of the cottage cheese would cover the cost of building the entire farm. Knowing perfectly well that these cunning tricks deceived no one, the older brother carried on cold-bloodedly stuffing the promissory notes into his pocket without batting an eyelid, then got on his motorbike and rode off to the notary public to get them witnessed, apparently without the slightest concern about what might stand behind the mute assent of his younger brother, who never checked anything, never tried to challenge anything, never paid any attention to the numbers and the letters that his hand traced out on the scraps of paper, just as though they were nothing to do with him at all.

The house was completely finished in mid-September; in addition he had knocked up two strong sheds out of sound beams and boards, after demolishing and clearing away the shed that had been knocked together in a hurry, built a new kennel for his dog and spread three truckloads of white river sand over the yard. And then, without even bothering to dust off the wood shavings and whitewash, without bothering to take a shave or at least scrape the scabby dirt off his gloomy face, he went down to the post office and sent off a telegram to Djezkazgan with just one word in it – 'Come' – then paid and went out without saying a word; the plump female telegraph operator said, 'He might at least open his mouth, the rotten devil.' The woman who took his telegram said, 'You heard for yourself, I kept asking him over and over again, and he just nodded or shook his head.' A third woman said, 'Who did he send the telegram to?' The one who took the telegram said, 'Mrs Baskakov,' and she said, 'Must be his wife, or maybe a sister-in-law.' The plump woman said, 'What would he be doing with a wife, the rotten devil?' The one who took the telegram said, 'But his name's Baskakov, isn't it?' The third woman said, 'That's the first time I've ever heard what his name is,' and then she said, 'We'll see soon enough,' and the plump woman said, 'Not that soon,' and she said, 'It's a long way from Djezkazgan.'

His wife and daughter arrived at the beginning of October. Before their arrival he'd managed to buy a few pieces of furniture: a table and chairs, beds, a pair of bedside lockers and a marked-down dresser with a set of shelves for dishes thrown in, which made it clear he'd had money from the moment he arrived and he simply hadn't wanted to pay cash for the building materials, preferring to write out promissory notes. What's more, in one of the sheds he built a partition out of unplaned laths, spread straw on the floor and bought a pig on the same day that he scattered the straw on the floor and set up a crudely cobbled together trough, although he could have bought a pig cheaper two days earlier from his neighbour, but hadn't because there was no trough yet, although it only took him an hour to knock one together, and because there was no straw spread on the floor, although it only took him five minutes to spread it. When two weeks had gone by since he sent the telegram, he began walking to the shop in the morning, to the place where the bus from the station stopped, and standing there silently, not greeting anyone, a little to the left of the door of the shop, with his felt hat with the broad, drooping brim pulled down over his eyes, chewing on a yellow straw, clean-shaven, decently dressed, wearing carefully cleaned shoes. No one had ever seen him like that and people who came to call in to the shop automatically smiled at him, assuming the man had changed his essential nature in the same way as he'd changed his appearance, but when they entered the critical zone of the radiation emitted by his personality, just like before they felt a confusion in their thoughts and an inexplicable weakness in every part of their

bodies, as though the living fibres of their muscles had suddenly come unglued and were no longer bound to each other,
like a cascade of dry hair or an unbound sheaf of wheat, and
they hurried by on legs of cotton-wool to escape the reach of the
baleful influence of the motionless figure frozen in an attitude of
imperturbable waiting. He came to meet the bus for two days,
but they only arrived on the third. They let all the passengers go
past in order not to hinder them with their baggage, and got off
the bus last. She was a tall, slim woman with a pale, beautiful
face, wearing a white dress: 'It's quite incredible,' said the schoolteacher, who was present and was the only man there she hadn't
struck dumb by her very appearance. 'Quite incredible,' he said,
'that anyone can emerge looking so clean and beautiful from
that rusty, dusty old washtub.' The woman was followed out by
a pretty girl of fourteen or fifteen in a beige skirt, brown blouse
and brightly coloured headscarf knotted under her chin so that
it concealed her cheeks up to the corners of her tender pink
mouth. The girl was carrying bags stuffed to the very limit and
the slim woman had two battered suitcases. Then the teacher
took a step towards the woman with the clear intention of helping her, but his glance clashed with the young girl's, and after
clashing glances with her he distinctly heard a clear crystal ring-
ing tone, like when two glass objects collide; he turned his head
towards the woman, but suddenly found himself in the position
of a man who wants to take a step forward but is pulled up
short by a noose thrown over his neck, and then he looked
towards the girl, for she was on the side where the invisible
noose originated, and he saw her slowly shake her head, pointing with her eyes to the motionless figure of a man in a felt hat,
who had been waiting for them to arrive for three days and now
that they were here had not moved from the spot; and the
woman with the two suitcases set off straight towards him. Only

then did the inhabitants of the village finally realize she was actually his wife. The schoolteacher said, 'Yes,' and he said it because it was simply his duty to say something, because he was the only one who knew how to speak properly, by virtue of his profession, and he said, 'I hope at least she's heard the sound of his voice,' and then he said, 'At least before the wedding.'

And yet, even after being convinced by their own eyes that his wife not only existed, but was young and beautiful, they were prepared to accuse their own sight of every possible crime for having played such an absurd trick on them, because they could not imagine him any other way than sleeping on the bare earth beside his dirty grey dog, and apart from that, they were obsessed by the question of whether this woman felt what they felt when they came close to him, or whether perhaps she was mad, so that confusion in her thoughts was her natural condition, and the weakness in every part of her body was a consequence of a different illness, which could have been cured in the past if not for the constant close association with him, which rendered the illness chronic. While they thought furiously, guessing wildly, the schoolteacher, munching on an apple, said, 'Now they'll go home and she'll mix him up a pudding batter,' and he said as he thoughtfully watched them go, 'I saw him buy flour yesterday.' Someone said, 'So what's the answer, is she crazy then?' The teacher said, 'She's not crazy,' and he said, 'The answer is that we're all crazy.' They didn't believe him and they were all about to object, all of them together, only they could see the teacher wasn't going to listen to them, maybe because he wasn't from those parts, whereas they were the very earth itself, and being the local earth, it was their business to know about everyone who walked on it. They watched them go, and they walked along the dusty road paved with cobblestones, then turned on to a dirt road, where their steps became soundless in the dust as thick and soft as moss, and they walked towards the new house in order to live there through the older brother's good offices, and their daughter walked ahead, guessing the way, astonishing everyone with her eyes as yellow as fermented honey that could restrain a man more powerfully than a noose. Afterwards they saw them often, but without Baskakov, who could quite easily walk past his wife or daughter when he met them on the street in the regional centre without saying a single word – it obviously never even entered his mind to talk to them until it was really necessary, simply on the grounds that one of them was his wife and the other was his daughter, just as it would never have entered anyone else's head to talk to the darkness of a well or the scent of a flower-bed; only if they themselves went up to him and stood in front of him, wanting to ask him something, to find out whether they ought to buy this or that in the shop, would he sometimes speak, but somehow as though he wasn't really speaking at all, just moving his lips, and not a single crease in his dark, gloomy face was either shortened or lengthened. If he happened to look at them at the same time, which happened very rarely, at least out on the street, in the sight of strangers, then he looked in the same way as he looked at the house he had built, as though he had built both of them just like the house, only a long time ago, following the designs and drawings as he assembled the bones and the cartilage into the skeleton, stringing on the sinews, veins and muscles, setting the blood in motion and coating the products of his labours with skin, and now thanks to him they were able to move, see, hear, breathe, and he couldn't understand what else they wanted from him. They were both irreproachably fine, not even by the strictest of standards did they possess a single flaw, unless you counted the burn mark on the daughter's cheek; this fiery brand was concealed by the bright-coloured headscarf, but after everybody already knew about it, the old women began claiming that the colour of the girl's eyes had betrayed what the bright-coloured headscarf concealed, because if fire once touches a child's face at the age when the eyes are still capable of changing colour, they turn yellow for the rest of the child's life and light his or her dreams with the pale lemon light of conflagration.

The older brother came to see Baskakov five times in the space of six months and cold-bloodedly demanded payment against the promissory notes, threatening in a flat, colourless voice to charge interest every month. These visits began three months after Baskakov found himself a job, but it was only on his fifth visit that the older brother announced that in two months' time he would be obliged to apply to the court and demand payment against the promissory notes under the law, and afterwards, as he said, he would auction the house off and in that way receive the money due to him from the new owner immediately after the inventory commission; to settle up before the deadline set by the older brother – that is, in two months – was quite obviously impossible, and he'd set the deadline in the certain knowledge that on those terms Baskakov wouldn't even bother to start paying him back, because it was pointless. There they sat on the hard chairs in one of the rooms of the new house, facing each other across the new round table covered with a check tablecloth, at first glance a pair of mindless dummies, in actual fact unforgiving enemies of the same blood who had always nurtured above everything else a cold mutual hatred that was carefully concealed, hidden away somewhere deep in the hollows of their eye sockets, smouldering in the ashes of sedition; they sat there, looking at each other. And then Baskakov said to him in an absolutely expressionless voice, 'I'll pay you everything in full, but over two years, as we agreed.' The older brother said, 'There's no mention of any two years in the promissory notes,' and he said, 'I need the money urgently.' Baskakov said, 'I'll pay you in full, but over two years,' and he said, 'Over two years, don't forget,' and then in the same voice, without any trace of expression, as though he wasn't saying anything but simply moving his lips, he said, 'And if you do take me to court, I'll kill you.'

The older brother's fifth visit, however, prompted some serious reflection that was followed by something akin to enlightenment, which nonetheless led to nothing and simply couldn't have led to any effective action, at least not just at present, apart from the sudden realization as he sat on the porch at midnight that his older brother didn't want the money for the promissory notes – that is, of course he wouldn't have turned it down if he could think of some way of extorting it, but the most important thing for him was a house that was built for nothing and registered in someone else's name. Baskakov had been used as a decoy, a fictional owner who could be deprived of his property at any time because he was in a position of legal vulnerability, powerless, pinned up against the wall by his own promissory notes. The older brother wanted the house, Baskakov couldn't see any other motive for him to make demands that were clearly impossible to meet. As for the matter of the additional twenty per cent over and above the state price for the building materials – in all probability that was a diversionary tactic that the older brother had hoped would convince Baskakov he had a personal financial interest in the deal, which would not have been so obvious without the twenty per cent profit, because no one could know for certain whether he'd paid his own money for the building materials or acquired them through various dubious manoeuvres, such as exchanging bricks for roofing slate, planks and cement, but that didn't matter very much now, just as the goals and sub-goals, secret hopes and dark intentions by which the older brother had been guided did not matter much, since for Baskakov the limits of Baskakov's interests were the limits of everything.

It happened in summer, about eight months after her mother got her passport back from the village soviet with the local authority's stamp in it and about a month after she, who didn't have any passport at all, was first seen in the company of the strapping lad who lived in the next village and had worked until recently as a loader at the margarine factory but had left that job and immediately found work as a loader at the brick factory. However, she clearly didn't enjoy her meetings with him all that much, or perhaps the burn mark on her left cheek made her feel shy, but one way or another, she was not the one who sought these meetings, and when she met him on her way home from school or from the cinema, which she occasionally visited with a group of girls her own age, who immediately left the two of them alone whenever he appeared, to judge from her pale face – if women's faces can be trusted at all – she felt nothing at all apart from mute inner torment. He walked calmly along beside her, tall and broad-shouldered, encased from head to toe in an impenetrable armour-plating of powerful muscles, and if his open shirtfront had not revealed a hairy chest, you might have thought he was wearing a suit of armour under his clothes, or at least a bulletproof waistcoat. However, that was only a first impression, which was dispelled on closer inspection, because from closer up you could see how smoothly and softly the skin rippled across the immense muscles, as smoothly and softly as the water in mountain rivers ripples over the smooth, round stones, and he moved just as smoothly and softly, but every movement was filled with the invincibility of water, the seeming calmness of current which disappeared without trace immediately the river-bed began to run downhill. He was twenty-five years old, but to look at he could have been all of thirty; he never walked as far as their house, always saying goodbye about two hundred metres away from it – he evidently realized that he would achieve his goal more quickly by not going against her wishes. But one time, when rumours about them were already frothing in bitter foam on the lips of the tight-laced villagers, he saw her to the very gate and the thing that she had been afraid of all this time happened: Baskakov came out of the house and began walking unhurriedly towards them. He opened the gate and without looking at the lad he turned a gaze of miserly, cold curiosity on his daughter and surveyed her in cold silence for a long minute, evidently trying to determine which would freeze first, a woman or time, and then he said calmly, 'Get off home.' When he was left alone with the lad, his head barely reaching up to the other's shoulder and his gaze level with his chest, Baskakov suddenly raised his hand and prodded the lad in the stomach with a dark, firm, straight finger, pressing back the mighty muscles as easily as though they were curtains of gauze, and said without the slightest expression, 'Don't let me see you with her again,' then he waited for a moment without taking his finger away, and said, 'That's all.'

For a long time in the village they couldn't figure out how, after Baskakov's warning, the lad could have decided to risk doing what he did afterwards with Baskakov's daughter in the pine forest – he lived on the same land as they did, it nurtured their muscles with the same strength and the same weariness, he breathed the same air as they did, inhaling resolution and exhaling irresolution, he drank the same water with an after-taste of grass and an after-taste of roots, but even so he decided to commit violence against a being whose immunity was inviolably guaranteed by Baskakov's very blood, by his sixteen years of sacred work and lastly, by the spectral seal of his ownership. It happened at noon on a cloudless, baking hot August Sunday, when the temperature of the air exceeded the critical level for the human body, when the inhabitants of the village, whose brains were boiling inside their skulls as though they were sealed into pressure-cookers, were awaiting some incomprehensible happening such as the orange mirage that had visited their skies five years previously in the exhausting heat of just such an August day, and which afterwards was described in full detail in the district newspapers of the region. And so, after the four-teen-year-old cowherd had driven his herd of cows, so stupefied by the heat that they refused to graze, through the village, kick-ing them under the ribs with his firm, round heels, they saw Baskakov's daughter and her broad-shouldered admirer, who had scorned her father's ban, sneak into the pine forest for a seri-ous talk. And only an hour later she was running towards the village from the direction of the pine forest on filthy, stiff, unbending legs scarcely able to support her, as though impelled on her way by the force of a single initial shove or impulse, in a torn, dirty dress with the stains of crushed black berries on its back, with a bleeding scratch on her face and pieces of bark, pine needles and moss tangled in her tousled hair. At the same time as his raped daughter came flying into the house with the firm intention of never leaving it again and collapsed there in the black emptiness of despair, making no attempt to conceal what had happened from her mother, Baskakov, dressed for autumn, despite the appalling heat, which was not capable of melting the internal deposits of ice in his soul, with his felt hat pulled down over his eyes, was installing home-made drain-screws at the end of the vegetable garden, among the tall swamp-rushes and sedge. He lowered the drain-screws into the deep, narrow trenches half-filled with putrid green water, dug to prevent the bog from flooding and washing away the plants set in the plots at the end of the vegetable garden during the spring rains, and with his lips sullenly clamped together, he thought about his older brother. Leaning down over the trenches in a rustling of dry reeds, catching a sharp scent of pond scum and fish, he was thinking: What has that son of a bitch thought up now? And he thought: I know for sure he must have thought up something because he hasn't shown up here for a month and a half with his lousy promissory notes. He had been thinking about his brother constantly, ever since the time when he sat out on the porch at midnight after his brother's fifth visit and realized his brother wanted the house; and in his pondering, in his implacable, solitary obduracy, he tried to work out all the possible variations, all the possible routes his brother might be following in order to take away the house built on a foundation of sweat and obstinacy, never doubting for a moment that a savage struggle lay ahead, a secret struggle concealed from others, between two beings of the same blood, born of the same woman, who had died long ago, but had predicted this struggle – an inhuman struggle, or rather a struggle of mutually exclusive phenomena – and of the same father, who had died long ago, hearing her predictions, but unable to detect in his sons' childish games any glimmer of their barely discernible, obstinate opposition to their mutual kinship. After they became adults they were unable to conceal it, despite the reticence and taciturnity typical of both of them, and it is quite possible that they would have united for the first and only time in order to wring the neck of anyone who discovered their blood-kinship, publicized and exposed it to public comment in this village, to which they had each come on their own and at different times.

Baskakov was out of the house for about another hour, during which his wife managed to tear off all of her daughter's clothes, soak them in kerosene and burn them in the stove, and as well as that she dragged her bodily out of the house, washed her in cold water, dressed her in clean clothing, tied a headscarf on her head to conceal the scratch on her forehead, and put her to bed, so that when Baskakov entered the house he was greeted by a still, heavy silence in which every sound seemed to assume visible form and a shout would have burst into flames. He didn't say anything to his wife and she laid the table in silence and, it was only afterwards, when he had hung his hat on the coat-stand, washed his hands and sat down at the table, as she poured fresh milk into a tin mug, that she said to him, 'Our girl's fallen ill.' He just looked at her with one eyebrow raised and continued chewing without speaking. She said, 'It's this damned heat,' then she turned away to the cooker and said, 'She'll be over it by tomorrow,' and she said, 'It's this damned heat.' Once again he said nothing, eating in silence without taking his eyes off his plate, absorbed in thoughts of his older brother, and she didn't say anything else about it. Then he got up, pushing his plate away, and went through into the next room, where their daughter was lying under a light bedspread. He hesitated for a second in the doorway, but on seeing that she wasn't sleeping, he went over to the bed and looked at her white, exhausted face, put his hand on her forehead and said, scarcely even moving his lips, 'No temperature,' and he asked, 'What's wrong with you?' And she said, 'Nothing,' controlling the spasms in her throat, she said, 'Nothing.' And she said, 'I've got a headache.' He took his hand away and said, 'Sleep,' and then wearily, submissively she closed her eyes, but the moment he left the room her eyes were open again.

And later, in the early evening, when his wife was thanking God that this accursed day was drawing to a close, and pleading for the darkness to take away everyone's memories, Baskakov's older brother came to see him. They conversed quietly for five minutes, standing by the window, facing each other, then the older brother caught sight of Baskakov's wife and asked her, 'What's wrong with your daughter?' He asked in an even voice, 'Has something happened?' And she said, 'She's fine, she's sleeping,' and she said, 'She's not feeling well, nothing to worry about,' and then she said, 'She'll be just fine tomorrow.' The older brother stared hard at her and then he asked, 'Is that right?' And he looked at her and asked again, 'Is that right?' And he said, 'All right then.' As soon as the door closed behind him she asked Baskakov in a strange, dull, lifeless voice, 'What did he want here? What did he want?' And she asked dully and uncertainly, 'What did he tell you?' Baskakov said, 'He told me not to hurry with the repayments, he told me I could pay over three years,' and he said, 'He told me not to hurry.' Then she grabbed him by his jacket sleeve and, peering into his face, she asked almost in a whisper, convulsively breathing out the air that caught in her throat, 'Was that all?' And she asked again, 'Was that all?' He said, 'Yes, it was.'

Meanwhile in the village they were waiting to see what would happen, or rather how it would happen, for they were convinced that it would. They trod a closed circle of anticipation, gulping down the red-hot air of the August day which was the only nourishment most of them took that Sunday, and the same day Baskakov's neighbour, evidently in an effort to break open the closed circle by physical action, slaughtered a black goat, skinned it, freed its bones from the meat and put them into a canvas bag, and when his frightened and indignant wife asked him why he'd done it and what he wanted the goat's bones for, he said darkly, 'For that bastard's grave.' But even after doing all this, he was forced to admit he still hadn't succeeded in breaking open the closed circle of anticipation, and hadn't even succeeded in breaking out of it; and as Sunday sank into the hot darkness of night-time they wondered more and more often whether they hadn't imagined this day, whether it hadn't been a dream, a warning. However, when late in the night the schoolteacher, tormented by the insomnia customary among people of a creative bent, rose from his hateful bed and splashed a little pink port wine into a glass in order to settle his jangling nerves and then drank it as he stood at the window, he saw a dim point of light glimmering somewhere over by the pine forest, and at first he thought nothing of it, taking it for the lamp on the water tower, but soon he noticed that little by little the point was expanding, moving in the direction of the village with the speed of a person running; and he thought he recognized something familiar in the trajectory of the glowing figure, something he had seen just recently, and then he was horrified to make out the features of a female figure running, a flickering of shapely legs and a flickering of free-flowing hair, and then the glowing phantom of a female body, now life-size, flitted past his house just as Baskakov's daughter had flitted past at noon in her dirty, tattered dress. And then the schoolteacher fumbled for the matches on the windowsill, struck one of them with trembling hands and squinted in pain as he put it out against his tongue, firmly convinced that he would immediately wake up, but when he opened his eyes he was still standing there by the window, looking at a glass of pink port wine, holding the matches, with a burnt tongue and a taste of sulphur in his mouth.

It was the next morning before everyone finally realized that Baskakov's wife and daughter had somehow managed to hide what had happened from him, for it never even entered their heads that he could know everything and not do anything about it; and that same morning the old man Pal, who had forced his way through the thorns of a great multitude of years with youthful sportiveness, cheating death with his smell, a small, skinny man shrivelled up like a saxaul plant, with no faith in the indestructibility of the geometrical form of the circle, headed directly for its centre. He went to the sawmill where Baskakov worked and told him everything he knew to his dark, impassive face, then went back to the village without waiting for an answer, almost running into the daughter by the power-saw as she was bringing Baskakov his lunch. And she only needed a brief glance at her father's dark, impassive face to see something new that was still invisible to everyone else – a barely perceptible grey sprinkling of words, the dust of truth that had settled on his face, turning its wrinkles black, as though they were drawn in charcoal. And he looked at his daughter for a few moments as he prepared to go, and then he said, 'So,' and he said, 'So,' and then he strode off slowly between the stacks of planks and off the sawmill's land.

He walked away uphill – she could not even imagine her father walking downhill – steadily, without hurrying across the dark, tough grass, and every step he took was a precise repetition of the one before it, and from the back of his head she could see that he was looking straight ahead, but no higher than the level of his head, as though there was nothing higher, only things that were lower or, very rarely, on the same level; and in this primordial, indestructible, unhurried movement, in this measured, focused stride there was not the slightest trace of stubbornness, of a desire to get anywhere or get away from anywhere; she thought: How is it possible to stop this, how is it possible to prevent its arrival, its advent? He walked away up the hill, flattening the coarse grass into the ground with his iron steps, and it seemed to her that he was capable of walking on in exactly the same way through the forest, not bending the trees over but simply annihilating them with his weight, without halting for even a second, not the way a steel machine weighing many tonnes would do it, deafening the surroundings with its hysterical roaring, spinning its wheels in the soft earth, but in the way this silently moving object only one and a half metres in length but possessing the weight of a planet would do it.

He reached the entrance checkpoint of the brick factory half an hour before the end of the first shift, when it had already started raining, and he stood motionless to one side, under a flowering acacia, with his wide-brimmed hat pulled down over his eyes, dispassionately chewing on a thin yellow straw, his eyes fixed on the battered door of the checkpoint, devoid not only of impatience and anger, but even of anticipation, watching as the first group of tired and tipsy workers emerged from the factory, swapping idle comments; he paid no attention to them, carrying on waiting, staring at the checkpoint in the fine rain that was growing stronger – a solitary finger of fate; and it was only a continuation, an extension of that measured, never-ending work which he had begun in the moment when he first conceived the intention of building his first house, a continuation of that undeviating line of conduct which he had chosen as a youth, and which had led him to commit a crime in which he had seen no more than the logical outcome of the situation, and in losing his first freedom, had lost the first house he had built.

And then the lad came out through the checkpoint, tall and strong, with a face tanned by the sun and the wind, wearing a faded yellowish-white soldier's jacket with dark-green patches where the straps had been torn away from his powerfully slanting shoulders, and as soon as he saw Baskakov his hands went to his trouser pockets, and one hand pulled out a long *papyros* and stuck it into his small navel of a mouth, and then the other hand appeared with a box of matches. He stood under the overhang of the checkpoint entrance while he lit up, then turned away from Baskakov and walked off into the rain. Then Baskakov, without changing his position or spitting out the straw that was stuck to his lower lip, said in a loud voice, 'Hey you, lad!' – that was all he said, then he turned on his heels and set off without looking round, hearing the sound of steps behind him. The other asked as he walked along after him, 'Where to?' Then Baskakov stopped, gave a barely noticeable nod to the left and said, 'That poultry farm over there.' The other asked, 'And after that?' – trying as he asked to make sense of the expression in the empty, indifferent eyes staring out at him from under the wide brim of the black felt hat, as cold and unfathomable as steel rivets, lacking the faintest spark of life, or even its reflection, and he asked again, 'And after that?' Baskakov said, 'After that you'll get to see something new,' and he set off again. Forcing their way through the thick wet undergrowth of tall weeds, nettles and wild flowers, they came across an old cart lying on its side in the centre of a small, almost square clearing scattered with pieces of broken brick, and the lad stopped and said, 'I'm not going any further,' and he said, 'There's no point in trudging all the way to the poultry farm, we can talk things over here,' and he began swaying back and forth on the balls of his feet, and then he stretched the hole that looked as though it had been drilled in his face into a tight, narrow smile, still believing that they had come here to fight, still trusting in the indomitable strength of his arms and his back, swaying on the balls of his feet in the warm rain that falls in late summer but brings no coolness and quickly turns into a stifling, damp mist. He swayed on the balls of his feet, looking Baskakov over from head to toe, scarcely able to restrain the ruthless, devastating strength of the muscles that were almost bursting through the seams of his clothes, to restrain the explosion of his massive body that seemed capable of blasting aside the motionless figure in the wide-brimmed hat without even touching it. He stopped swaying on the balls of his feet the second he heard a sharp click of the kind that can be made by firm, powerful fingers demanding attention, but he knew it wasn't fingers, and he didn't hear the click with his ears – his ears had nothing to do with it, and even if they'd been stopped up with wooden bungs from wine barrels, he would have heard this click with his skin, just as the blind boy heard the steps at dawn – his skin allowed the sound through into his inner darkness and it penetrated without hindrance, like radiation, paralysing all the movements of his body, and through all the narrow channels polished smooth by his blood, death ran, more silent than electricity; and afterwards for just a split second he saw the fourteen centimetres of gleaming steel, untouched by the rain, protruding from the dark fist.

Baskakov set off towards the village through the pine forest filled with the noise of rain, feeling the soft, yielding earth under his feet, hearing the swishing of the thick, wet grass against the toes of his boots and thinking about himself. They caught up with him two hundred metres from the lake, where the pine trees were already growing thinner but were still as tall and straight as ever, only now they were wet on all sides from the rain. When he saw his older brother with them, he understood everything, but he didn't make a single unnecessary movement, and the expression on his dark, morose face, as set and motionless under the streaming drops of water as a tortoise's shell, didn't change at all, as though it couldn't change, as though it hadn't changed since he was born, but had only been coarsened by the action of sun, time and wind. They ran towards him in the rain, weaving their way through the wet trunks of the pines, and looking at them he thought: Right, he thought: Right, so that's the way you decided to get me out of my house, and he thought: Right. He knew the most important thing now was to warn his wife not to leave the house no matter what, the most important thing was to tell her not to leave under any circumstances, not to move out of that house the way she had done to follow him when he was jailed the first time, because if the house was occupied by a solitary woman and her child, it wouldn't be so easy for him to get his hands on the house, even with his promissory notes, because the law was always on the side of the woman and the child, and he thought: I should have thought about that right from the start, and he thought: I should have known he was following me and the lad, that he had it all worked out, and he thought: He knew I'd kill him, he had three gundogs ready and waiting and set them off on the scent straight away, and he thought: Now he'll tell her to move out and she will, like the first time, because I didn't tell her anything. It was clear enough that as far as they were concerned the fact that he'd killed the lad was indisputable; they didn't even ask if he'd killed him. He stood between two militiamen, facing a young, energetic lieutenant standing beside a tall pine-tree, feeling the soft, yielding earth under his feet; he didn't look at his older brother, he looked at the lieutenant. The lieutenant said, 'What are you looking at?' The lieutenant was armed. He said to the lieutenant, 'I have to see my wife,' and he said, 'Just for a minute.' The lieutenant said, 'No.' He said, 'I have to see my wife'; his older brother said, 'And what else do you want?' The lieutenant said, 'You'll see her in court.' He said in an expressionless voice, 'I have to see her just for one minute.' The lieutenant looked at his older brother without speaking. The older brother said in a steady voice, 'He killed a man.' Then the lieutenant said, 'Come on, get moving,' signalling to the two militiamen, and they took hold of his arms just above the elbow, but he didn't budge from the spot, and they couldn't shift him. Raindrops ran slowly down his motionless face, trembling on his twisted lips and slanting chin. He looked past the lieutenant at his older brother. Then he licked his cold lips and said, 'Right, you bastard.' The lieutenant looked at the older brother and then at Baskakov. 'Right, you bastard,' said Baskakov, looking at his older brother. Then they led him away across the wet grass. He walked along between them, saying, 'Right, you bastard. Right.'

# Country of Origin

From his former life he still had the rumbling in his ears, but not as loud as it used to be, when the rumbling seemed to run through his entire body, setting his very bones, teeth and nails buzzing, not so all-pervading that it seemed as though the dark cavern of his body was collapsing in on itself, not the loud rumbling which made it impossible to hear what people were saying even when they spoke right into his ear. But then, a long time ago, he had told himself: It's the rumbling of my heart. And where previously he hadn't even been able to hear himself speak and only knew his own thoughts, now that he'd married the woman who'd picked him up at the railway station and brought him home and presented him to her mother, he was able to hear both of them as he tried to adjust, allowing intelligible speech inside himself, transforming other people's words into something physically palpable and feeling them on the skin of his face, like fluffy, almost weightless lumps of cotton wool. But he still hadn't managed to break the habit of yelling even when it was quiet in an attempt to shout above the rumbling of his own internal collapse, and his piercingly loud voice, bellowing out words which seemed less meaningful and more absurd the louder he yelled them, would make the window-panes rattle, turn clear water cloudy, set the ash in the stove quivering.

Maria's mother never did find out exactly what happened between them at the railway station, but like a miser she hoarded away in her memory every detail of the day when her daughter appeared with a man just one and a half metres tall whose clothes were no good for anything except maybe rag torches. She saw that day in the hypnotic trance of her sleepless nights throughout the entire seven years of life that were left to her, beginning from that same day; and she saw the main event of that day on her deathbed as she floated along, submerged in the slow, gentle current of dying, and her daughter and future husband one and a half metres tall floated along with her, frozen in her mind exactly as she had remembered them for all time, before they had time to grow close and do all the things they did later, the two of them standing silently in front of her as they readied themselves to tell her what they had decided without asking for her blessing.

It was only natural that what Maria had done didn't come as much of a surprise to those who knew her – and there were very many people who did; in other words, they'd been expecting something of the sort from her for a long time, especially just recently. They observed her gazing up inquiringly into the night sky and searching for her star, broadcasting the energy of her frenetic craving for motherhood out into the cosmos; and so they had no reason to doubt that the moment she discovered that star, or at the very latest the next morning, she would go out into the street with a net and ropes, catch the first man she came across, tie him up and drag him back into the house.

She brought him home on Wednesday, at eleven o'clock in the morning, and at half past eleven he was already standing naked in the yard, between the barn and the shed where the hay was stored, facing a large, deep basin full of warm water; his old clothes, folded neatly, lay to one side and later, when Maria had armed herself with a coarse birch bark scrubber and soap and bent him over the basin, lathering the absolutely white, almost hairless male body in dispassionate silence, from time to time he would strain his neck to catch a glimpse of his clothes and the chickens hovering around them. The entire, thoroughly executed procedure of washing took no more than half an hour, after which she dried him off with a fluffy towel, then picked up his old clothes and led him into the house, into the room which she had thought of as her own ever since she was sixteen, where a new set of man's clothes with the price tags still on them was laid out on the wide, virginal bed; a light cream-coloured shirt, dark pressed trousers with a crisp new belt already threaded through the loops, blue socks and a pair of shiny black shoes, all the things she had bought with slow, fastidious care from the age of twenty to the age of thirty-five in anticipation of inevitable married life, for an imaginary man of medium height and build. And she said to him, 'There you are!' And she said, 'These are your new clothes, put them on,' and then she went out, closing the door behind her and leaving him alone with the invisible scent of a woman's loneliness, which she thought should convince him that he was the first man here and would be the last, at least for as long as the room belonged to her.

He appeared behind her, arrayed in his new clothes, when she was standing at the cooker in the kitchen after having already checked the pockets of his old clothes before throwing them away, and not noticing his appearance or turning round she was holding a thick piece of paper folded over many times in one hand and in the other a dark rag with something wrapped in it. The next second the folded sheet of paper went flying into the rubbish pail and immediately, instantly, that very same second he yelled out, 'Stop!' And then again, almost without pausing, he yelled out, 'Stop!' And he dashed towards the rubbish pail and overturned it with a clatter on to the clean floor-rag, then cleared aside the potato peelings, chicken giblets and porridge-like sludge destined for the pigs, grabbed the edges of the frayed piece of paper with both hands and set about carefully shaking the filth off it, kneeling down on the ground beside the rubbish pail. Then, still not recovered from the shock, she said in a muffled voice, 'My God,' and she said, 'What is it?' And he yelled, straightening up but not getting up from his knees, 'What is it? What is it?' And grimacing crookedly with a face that was too small for such a large head, he yelled, 'It's my pedigree!' She stood there facing him with her mouth wide open in amazement, pale and still, never having heard of anyone apart from hunting dogs and Persian cats having a pedigree before, and when he'd shaken the slightly damp piece of paper clean he got up from his knees, awkward in clothes that weren't his size but not seeming to notice or be concerned about it, feeling as though his eardrums were bursting from the dreadful rumbling, and reaching out his hand quickly he grabbed the rag bundle and yelled, 'Give it to me!' Then he yelled, 'Right, then!' After that he went out and sat in the garden for a long time with his gaze fixed on the trunk of a plum tree, and his body shuddered to the stony blows of his heart and he muttered to himself under his breath, 'Damn it, damn it, don't let my ribs crack, don't let my ribs crack.'

But that same evening, when the rumbling in his ears had died down a little and his heart had quietened a little in his

chest, after he'd sat for a while by the window in the still twilight, he went over to the table and laid out the notorious frayed
sheet of paper, which proved to be old but still quite sturdy
Whatman paper a metre square, in front of Maria and told her to
call her mother. Then both women leaned down over the table
in the soft yellow light of the lampshade and their shadows fell
across numerous names set out in strict sequence with various
kinds of explanatory notes, even including height, and incomprehensible cabbalistic symbols, crosses and numbers, signs of
the zodiac and short, neat arrows indicating the blood line; and
if they had been able to understand the detail and grasp the
integral meaning of this tightly organized heraldic chart in
which one of them was due to occupy a space, they would have
seen the story of a gradually degenerating stock, evident in a
constant decline in height and an equally constant increase in
the incidence of illness among its members, for the founding
member was shown as a giant beside whose name there was not
a single denigratory symbol, not a single mark indicating the
slightest aberration in his mighty physical organism, nothing
but a sign of the zodiac and the figure ninety-nine, indicating the
number of years he lived. They stood for ten minutes leaning
over the table in complete silence with their eyes glued to the
clear lines of this lifeless picture, so that eventually they felt
they could actually see the frozen, sullen faces of all these people
hidden away behind the impenetrable masks of eleven surnames, and then he jabbed his finger at the very lowest of them,
jutting out in isolation from the dense ranks, and said, 'That's
me.'

And that was the only time he allowed them to lay eyes on the
origins of his blood line, but he himself laid out the sheet of
Whatman paper at least once a week and pored over it for hours
at a time, like an archaeologist journeying across the world with

the help of a map, stubbornly deciphering the symbols and looking for the markings that indicated heart disease. During those
hours the mother would invariably take the opportunity to tell
Maria, 'That man is a fugitive from the law,' and she would tell
her, 'You'll see.' And she repeated these words relentlessly, casting the yarn of her doubt on to the needles of her daughter's
inflexible character until her daughter finally exploded in a fit of
righteous indignation and shouted, 'Perhaps he is, I don't care!'
And then, with a crooked smile at her own thoughts, she said,
'I'm not the law, am I?' But her mother said to her, 'It's true, I can
tell it's true,' and then Maria looked her mother in the eyes and
for the first time she spoke out loud the only rule she had managed to derive from thirty-five years of life: 'There is only one
truth and that is that we live here and nowhere else, and this is
the only truth worth clinging to, this is the truth we must
believe in and everything else is lies, because everything else can
be turned inside out.'

Two days before he and Maria formalized their relationship in
law he bought a fairly new grey suit from the artist Pal's widow,
for a price that was more than modest, to wear at the wedding.
The widow told him beforehand, 'You ought to know that my
husband died in this suit.' Then he said to her, 'But I'm going to
live in it.' She said to him, 'Go on then,' and she said, 'Only
don't live like he did.' But on the eve of the wedding Maria,
seeing him transfer a dirty rag from the pocket of his shirt to the
pocket of his jacket, that same dirty rag with something tied up
in it, went up close to him and said, 'Wait,' and she held out a
small tobacco pouch she'd found in the drawer of the old sideboard among the worthless pre-reform money, threadbare
handkerchiefs and yellowed letters. He looked at her without
speaking and she said, 'Throw away that rag,' and she said, 'Put
everything in this pouch and carry it around with you if you

want to.' He looked at her, still without speaking, and then he unfolded the rag, which turned out to contain his passport, his army identity card, a small amount of money and two little bundles of cigarette paper. Pointing to the little bundles she asked him, 'What's in there?' Then he unwrapped the crackling cigarette paper slowly and carefully and she saw seven beautiful white teeth and a lock of hair, and she touched them with her finger and asked him, 'Are they your teeth?' He said, 'Yes,' and he told her, 'I lost these teeth when I was a child, and then different ones grew instead.' She smiled and he looked at her, and it was one of those rare occasions when his chest was filled with unbroken silence. She said, 'And this is a child's hair,' and he said, 'A seven-year-old child.' She asked, 'Is it your hair?' He said, 'No,' then he told her calmly, 'This is Idea's hair.'

And the day after the modest, unremarkable wedding he put on the well-ironed grey suit in which the artist Pal had died and went to the district employment office, where on hearing that he'd lost his employment record book but didn't know where, a middle-aged woman with a face as yellow as a melon, sitting in a square, brightly lit room with cacti and aloe plants on the peeling window-sills, began listing off jobs, glancing into the papers that lay in heaps on the lacquered surface of her desk. He sat there without speaking on a rickety stool, biting his nails stupidly, stupefied by the tedious, sleep-inducing voice which seemed to keep pronouncing the same word but in different ways, always offering him the same kind of work, only with different intonations. Drugged by the rustling of the sheets of paper, he only answered her once, when she offered him a job involving some kind of clerical scribbling and he said furiously, 'I hate shuffling papers about!' And finally she said, 'All right then,' and she asked him, 'What are you good for? What can you do?' And then without pausing for thought he said, 'Shoot.'

And so he got a job in a shabby, dirty shooting gallery on the market square, where in the space of only four days he introduced the most incredible good order, because he saw a profound meaning in it. Firmly convinced that he was finished for ever with his old hollow existence, he came to work at dawn and tinkered away with stubborn devotion in the cold hall of the shooting gallery until opening time, cleaning the air rifles and painting the little figures of animals and birds cut from thin sheets of iron, always using bright colours to make it easier for people with weak eyesight to hit the target. He replaced the dim light-bulbs that barely glimmered, and the hall of the shooting gallery became spacious and light; he constructed sturdy, stable benches for little children to stand on, and supports for the rifle barrels. At ten o'clock in the morning he opened the shooting gallery, took his seat in the booth with the narrow little window through which he handed out the pellets and sat there immersed in the healing waters of quiet happiness, hardly aware of the customers, hardly aware of his own hands taking the money and counting out the pellets, but catching every rustle of movement, every secret subterranean groan, for the beating of his heart no longer prevented him from hearing the world. This was the very time when people who met his gaze began noticing a calm, cold wisdom in his eyes and people who spoke with him were obliged to listen hard in order to catch his soft, tranquil voice. And in the evening, after thoroughly tidying the shooting gallery, he went home, pressing to his unmurmuring heart the tobacco pouch that contained seven white teeth and Idea's hair.

Meanwhile Maria's mother, whose ageing legs wreathed in swollen blue-green veins were like old demijohns and required warmth, began to feel a cold draught from her son-in-law's sharp movements, and during the first three months he was in the house this cold spread all the way through it, permeating the bricks of the walls. She began to feel a penetrating chill emanating from the painted floorboards and the table tops, a chill emanating from the cupboards, the mirrors and the sewing machine, and she began to notice she was dressing more warmly in the house than when she went out. The flies in the house disappeared, and the ones that missed their chance to fly away became drowsy and died as they did in late autumn; the holy crucifix that she invariably kissed stealthily before she went to bed became icy cold and she was haunted by the feeling that if she held the legs of the iron Christ to her lips any longer than a minute, she would have to use hot milk to prise them away from the crucifix, the same as it was all those years ago, when she'd touched the iron support of a swing with her lips on a cold frosty day. She said to Maria, 'Can't you feel it, the way your husband has turned the house into a cold cellar?' And she asked her, 'How can you sleep with him if even in the next room I feel like I'm climbing into a snowdrift when I go to bed?' But Maria didn't notice anything, she moved around the cold house like a burning match, bearing within her the infernal flame of a invincible love that could not merely melt ice but even set it alight like pure alcohol; and her mother said to her, 'My God, we'll die of cold here on these frozen-stiff sheets.'

But although the mother's fears were greatly exaggerated, sometimes she noticed things about her son-in-law that would be enough to upset anyone; for instance, she saw with her own eyes how he held a small piece of butter in his hand for at least five minutes, and not only did the butter not melt, it actually became even harder, and after that she became firmly convinced that the liquid flowing in his veins was not blood, but the fluid used to circulate cold in refrigerators. And as winter approached she told Maria more and more often, 'I'm cold,' and she said, 'I'm freezing, chilled to the bone.' Maria told her, 'It's your own stupid ideas that are making you cold.'

But the day came when Maria came home from work to find her mother sitting on her packed luggage. She stopped in front of her and asked in quiet anger, 'What's this?' Then she said even more quietly, 'Where do you think you're going?' And her mother, staring into the corner where the half-empty coat-rack hung, said distantly, 'Today I dreamed that our cow froze to death.' Maria said, 'O my God,' and she said, 'You're always dreaming about something or other,' and then she asked, 'Where do you think you're going?' Her mother said, 'I'm going to live with my sister.' Maria asked, 'Why?' Her mother stared silently into the corner with her wrinkled lips pressed tightly together. Maria shouted, 'Why? Can you tell me why?' Then her mother said, 'It's warm there.'

He was there when her mother left, but he didn't make anything much of it, not wishing to disturb the balance established in his organism between load and support, valuing above all else this dead equilibrium, which was only possible within the structure that had been systematically built up inside him since he took the job at the shooting gallery, where from one day to the next he maintained ideal order in a calm, measured, relentless manner, never being parted from his cleaned air rifles and brightly coloured little figures of doomed animals for longer than a night, never removing the seven white teeth and the lock of hair from his heart. In the meantime he didn't notice the dry, infectious chill with which he had filled and infected the house, he didn't notice the irreversible process of deterioration that had even seeped into the stone and established itself in the walls which sheltered the silently raging flame of his wife's love, born of extreme loneliness and relentless time.

And after her mother left, his style of life remained just as measured and invariable, apart from a few innovations to do with his job in the shooting gallery, such as shooting at live mice, a trick which he had already been performing with an infallible, supernatural precision for a fortnight, ever since a mouse that wandered into the hall of the shooting gallery had given him the idea of animating the overly mechanical shooting game by introducing into it the brutal excitement of a pseudo-deadly game from which an old ancestor of his had derived sweet, feverish pleasure in the previous century when he hunted wild boar. In all probability, this was the same man to whom he owed his own faultless eye, lightning reactions and ruthless finishing, whose blood predominated in his own, whose instincts dwelt in his body, imparting electric swiftness to his limbs; that man had given him everything except scale. The scale of the man and the scale of his quarry. In any case, unlike Maria and her mother, he could not fail to spot the obvious degeneration of his line as he pored for hours at a time over the sheet of Whatman paper, his gaze taking in all the surnames of the modern decay, recalling everything that he was capable of recalling, exposing the white bones of half-forgotten legends, all the while experiencing the feeling a man experiences when he looks the wrong way through binoculars. But even knowing all of this, he had recently begun to believe fervently in a repeat flowering, like lobelias or begonias. He had convinced himself that in this world the final degeneration of a blood line already verges on its regeneration and is sometimes so intimately bound to it that the actual moment of transition is not visible to an outsider. So great was his certainty that he had a premonition of bearing a seed capable of giving the world the first shoot of a great and powerful line. One day he set a garden ladder up against the house and clambered into the attic to hide the paper there, to bury it like something shameful and incriminating; and in the dim rays of the grey light filtering into the attic through the little window covered with cobwebs, moving slowly and clumsily in the thick wood-dust, he hid the sheet of Whatman paper between the rough-hewn beams and heaped old revolutionary journals over the spot, in order to imitate the flowers of the field and bury the grim past for ever. After that he was never parted from the tobacco pouch and its contents, that modest, almost weightless reliquary, which in his mind weighed as much and meant as much, or even more, than dams and mausoleums, and he devoted all of his energies to hunting mice, for which purpose he constructed a plexiglass box with a spring-loaded mechanism for the door, which was primitive, but nonetheless worked without a hitch, using pieces of stale cheese as the bait.

From time to time Maria's mother would visit her. As she entered the house she would ask in the doorway if her daughter's husband was home and when she was told no she would wander round the rooms with a shuffling gait, and her wrinkled, tragic face reflected a feeling of amazement. One time Maria asked her, 'What are you looking so surprised about?' Her mother, smelling the thick scent of decay given off by the walls, said quite sincerely, 'I'm surprised this house hasn't collapsed yet.' In a spirit of malicious despair she rubbed her dry lips together as she painstakingly counted up the cracks and the yellow patches of damp on the ceiling that weren't there before, noting every patch that was peeling or covered with voracious mould; after the shock of the blackened silver forks and spoons she almost needed resuscitation, for she had been convinced that silver could not turn black, and if the noble metal had turned black it meant there was no material in the world which would not crumble to dust at her son-in-law's touch, except perhaps for her own daughter. On one of her visits she told Maria resolutely, 'You have to take that blasted tobacco pouch away from him and throw it into the bog with everything inside it!' Maria asked coldly, 'What for?' Her mother said, 'Why does he have to carry his lost teeth and that hair around with him everywhere?' Maria said, 'That's his business.' Her mother asked, 'Whose hair is it?' Maria said, 'I think it's a woman's hair.' Her mother asked, 'What woman?' Maria said in a muted voice, 'A woman by the name of Idea.' Then her mother said with contemptuous pity, 'An idea isn't a woman,' and then she said, 'An idea is an idea.'

From the moment he got rid of the Whatman paper and buried the biological map of his family line, together with the sound commonsense of the processes of life, under heaps of old revolutionary journals, he was sure there was not and could not be any other hand but his own capable of revitalizing and continuing that list of names hidden away in the attic; time stood still for him, and he began thinking seriously about immortality. Three weeks later, when he was approaching the essence of immortality by basing his approach on time standing still while the body carried on moving, when his consciousness was about to go splurging into emptiness, he suddenly had a dream about black horses hurtling along, and time began moving again. He woke up with a heavy head and set off for work with a bitter presentiment of disaster. And that was the day when they told him they were closing the shooting gallery down for the winter. And then for the first time in three months he heard the deafening sound of his own heart and he instantly forgot his pseudo-deadly game and his reflections on corporeal immortality and went dashing out of the shooting gallery, push-ing the light door open with his foot, and he ran through the howling desert of time, at first quickly, then ever more slowly, until his feet began tripping over each other under the excessive weight of his small, vibrating body. And then he collapsed and his lips touched the hard, indifferent earth and a black flower blossomed in his brain.

The old man who delivered cans of milk on his creaky cart, lashing at his bald chestnut nag with a hemp rope, took him to the red-brick hospital, where two orderlies picked him up, still trembling and smelling of the milk spilled by the potholes, and carried him away. In the ward they undressed him and put him on a sloppily made bed and he lay there delirious until the evening, a drowned man on the ocean floor, trying to comprehend the black blossom in his brain and why some bastard had decided it was necessary to deprive him of the work he loved for the idiotic reason that it snowed every other day. In the evening Maria came to see him, but all of her words, her painful anxiety, her broken movements, even her very existence, were drowned out by the rumbling roar of his heart, along with the existence of all the other people living together with him in this country.

Subsequently everything that the local doctors and the doctors summoned from the big city did to him, scrutinizing the X-ray photographs of his soul through the white rays of his ribs in their countless offices and cubicles, those photographs of his rumbling heart, where they were horrified to discover a lead bullet embedded deep in the muscle of the left ventricle, overgrown with a mass of fibrous tissue and driving the blood through the vessels together with the working muscle; and examining his puny, white, hairless chest in the hope of discovering an opening from the bullet that lay in his heart, but not finding anything even remotely similar apart from a nipple – everything that they did to him they did in order to illuminate his dark brain and reveal the true, the only meaning of the incomprehensible symbol above the name of the hunter of wild boar, which had been unjustly forgotten, but which signified that this man had lived half his life with a bullet in his heart, which was lodged there during a hunt, either by accident or with malicious intent, and now, seven generations later, the same fate had overtaken his descendant, but from birth, without any shot being fired. Everything they did to him, they did in order to remind him that the cycle of winter is accorded as much time as the cycle of summer and the cycle of rumbling as much time as the cycle of silence, and the cycle of degeneration as much time as the cycle of regeneration; it is not slow, but neither is it quick. They would come to him and ask, 'What do you feel inside you?' Every time they asked him, 'What do you feel inside you?'

And unknown to them their actions achieved their goal on that night when, lost in a deep sleep, he had a vision of the forest of that ancient hunt and a man rising from the ground. In the morning he asked the nurse to bring him his clothes and she asked him, 'Why?' He said, 'I'm going home,' and he said, 'I understand everything now.' But they wouldn't let him go and then he waited until Maria came and told her to bring the grey suit from home. And that day, arrayed in a dead artist's suit, his small fist clutching the tobacco pouch containing seven white teeth and Idea's hair, he faced the senior physician and said calmly, 'I'm going home,' and he said, 'I understand everything now.' The doctor said, 'Don't do that.' He said, 'I'm going.' The doctor squinted at him and asked, 'What do you feel inside you?' And then he said firmly, 'Certainty.'

# On Going to Hell

## 1

In three days the special train covered one thousand eight hundred kilometres.

They were all as drunk as cobblers apart from the driver, but they never saw him. During the long stops in sidings on the approaches to the big towns, when the special train let express trains and passenger trains past, they would get out of the only sleeping carriage, most often at night, and go wandering among the low steel flatcars carrying combine-harvesters, among the goods trains with their tankers of petrol, oil, bitumen and natural gas. They tried to sell the local people canned meat, salami and condensed milk, or exchange them for home brew; they smoked and talked, sobering up a bit in the wind; they watched the railway workers moving slowly along the trains in their orange overalls, checking and greasing the axle bearings.

No one ever knew, or if they did, they'd long since forgotten, how the black cat ended up in the carriage; they treated him very politely because he was black, and those who fed him, giving up the best bits of their food, were quite convinced that they would never be derailed, never be maimed in a fight, never be made a fool of by a woman, and those who didn't feed the cat avoided looking him in the eye as they ate. The cat moved from one sleeping compartment to another, tumbling round their feet like a black ball, and when it began to get dark he would jump up on to the little table, arching his back, easing his way between the empty bottles to a spot closer to the window and sit there right through the night. The light of the towns slanted down on him, igniting a predatory yellow flame in his eyes, and afterwards, when the towns and the stations were left behind, he sat there motionless, submerged in the gloom of the nocturnal forests and fields.

Every evening the drunken conductor wandered through the carriage, bumping against the ends of the seats as he went and mumbling continuously, 'No light tonight. No light tonight. No light tonight.'

At first they used to say the conductor was just a new stage in their misfortunes, the conductor was like the head of state, but then they stopped paying any attention to him. And quite often the conductor would say, 'Look at me. Forty-five days a swine, forty-five days a king.'

In the morning they woke up dirty, unshaven and puffy-faced, and rubbed their dried lips together as they struggled to utter a curse, looked at each other through inflamed eyes and said, 'Wake that guy up,' unable to bear the sight of anyone hiding himself away in sleep from the carriage that reeked of stale tobacco and sweat, from the real, hellishly slow movement of time, for any longer than they had been able to.

The first to wake up was always Shadrin, one of the few who washed himself, a large swarthy man of forty-three, sullen and untalkative, like a colonel whose entire regiment has been killed in battle; when he was furious his glance stopped up mouths better than a wooden gag. He wasn't liked, he was too much like a big, strong bull turning his head in silent fury and peering around in search of the man who was destined to kill him. They kept out of his way and heaped insults on him behind his back, the way people heap insults on Jesus Christ; the black cat did likewise, its feline intuition sensing that his race was already run.

Shadrin didn't wake anyone else, he got washed and went into the lobby of the carriage, lit a blowlamp, put it under a rusty, lopsided little trivet and boiled up enough extract of chicken soup to last him for lunch and supper – he was the only one on the train, apart from the black cat, who ate three times a day. Then he handed on the trivet and the blowlamp to one of the others who shared a compartment with him: Bragin, Zhigan or Ratalov.

There was only one blowlamp between all of them, and the last in line breakfasted in the evening.

On the fifth day, when they had almost passed the Urals – the tall grey hills, the shallow-sided mountains frozen beneath the rustling of the evergreen fir forests, the red canyons, the long dark tunnels, the little white houses on the shallow slopes, so fragile and unprotected that it seemed the sound of a human voice could sweep them away and leave no trace behind – Shadrin's old ulcer opened up.

He tossed about heavily on the top bunk, gasping for breath in the dense cigarette smoke, as though he was bound to a spit over a fire, then he got up without saying a word, stuffed a blanket into his knapsack, with several tins of condensed milk, some left-over lumps of butter, a spoon, a flask of water and some matches, waited till the next halt and got out of the carriage. The men who were helping the drunken conductor fill up the water tank saw him climb on to one of the steel flat-cars and get into his own truck, hunched over with his pale lips tightly clenched.

Now the special train has another three days to travel, with frequent stops in sidings, and Shadrin will spend all that time in his truck, lying on the hard seat under a thin blanket riddled with holes, looking out at the autumnal forest through the cloudy glass streaming with rain, growing numb at night with cold when he's burned all the petrol, and then he will feel the cold dulling the pain in his stomach and remember.

He was a boy, lying behind the sand quarry with his legs broken, lying on the cold, hard earth, and they brought the midwife and the driver of a one-and-a-half-tonne truck to attend to him. They lifted him up and carried him to the road, and the driver asked, 'Hey, fatso, why isn't he yelling?' and the midwife said, 'Because it's cold.' Somehow they got him into the truck and drove him off to the hospital. He still couldn't feel anything and it was only in the dressing-room, when his legs were already bandaged from the calves up to the hips and they began to plaster them with warm plaster of Paris, that he wanted to howl out loud and he wanted to be somewhere far away, in the snow.

And then, hunched over on the seat, Shadrin will wait for the cold of the night, which will numb the spasms of pain; falling asleep, waking up, just lying there.

That woman, the old crone, whatever her name was, spoke in a quiet, indistinct voice, like a sparrow rustling its wings. 'She wrinkled up her crumpled dishcloth of a face – I was delivering her – and said, "Listen to me, you young whelp." She was laid out in the old professor's house, in a room with ceilings four metres high and old furniture covered with carvings, on a tall, luxurious bed, thrashing about under my hands, as wet and slippery as a frog from sweat and all night long she couldn't do it, she just couldn't. Early the next morning she began yelling so loud that plaster began falling off the ceiling, and in the next room the old pictures fell off the walls, and the crystal clinked and jingled, then she began cursing and I told her, "Don't you dare curse, you bitch, your son's going to be born lucky," and she lay there streaming with sweat and cursing away like hell, and said, "I should think so!" And she yelled, "Wipe my snot away." She gave birth at noon, and you looked like you'd been bayoneted, covered in blood, and under your arms and between your legs the flesh was raw. I held you by the left leg, and you hung there upside down without making a sound; I slapped you and I couldn't tell if you were alive or dead. Then when you came to life and fell asleep for the first time out in the big wide world, we listened to the professor, who had drawn up your horoscope to the accompaniment of the screams of childbirth, and the light of a non-existent star promised to endow you with a powerful, clear mind, protect you against wars, illnesses and prisons, promised to show you a safe path, an easy life free of cares, blessed with beautiful women born under the signs of Sagittarius, Virgo, Aries and Libra and beautiful, healthy children. Back then I used to know quite a lot about horoscopes and I knew the horoscope compiled by the professor was lies from beginning to end; no doubt he wanted to engrave his non-existent horoscope on your non-existent memory, as a guide to action, but your genuine astral horoscope foretold nothing good, and as for your arboreal horoscope, the section on illnesses said that a person born under a lucky star will die in childbirth.'

In the mornings, as he eats half a tin of condensed milk and a piece of butter, Shadrin will search for a way to fight off his spasm of hunger – biting his lips, twisting his fingers, stabbing himself with a knife, lying on his back and staring up into the air.

Previously a stubborn, vicious and hard-headed man, his grandfather had come back from the war at the age of thirty-six a lunatic, or whatever the proper name is for someone who is normal by day and crazy by night. By day he was as modest and unassuming as the light and never spoke in places where there were icons, but at night he got out of bed without waking up or making a sound and, guided by the darkness, went out into the garden and burned off the dry grass under the nut-tree, dug over the earth and lay face down on the burnt grass, doubled up as though he had stomach cramps, and said, 'All right. What should I do?' Then he went back into the house and his hair smelled of smoke and his hands smelled of fresh earth. They told him what he was doing at night; at first he didn't understand a thing, and when he did understand he didn't want to talk about it, and then later he told them in a voice devoid of pain or anger, 'They simply didn't have time to take me with them, they kept on running further and further away, with the bullets lighting up the way, and I was lying at the bottom of a bomb crater with my belly torn open, stuffing the hot guts back in, swearing and cursing, yelling out in pain and anger, because I knew they wouldn't come back for me. I bit my lips, twisted my fingers, stabbed myself with a knife, I growled and swore, because I thought as long as you keep on fighting, you're still alive. It was a long time before I realized I was a dead man, and then I resigned myself to it and realized how stupid and petty I was, and then I began believing in God and said to him, "All right. What should I do?" The wind carried away the pain and the anger, and an hour later they came back for me.' A dog started barking outside, someone had arrived. And the old woman said, 'All right. Where are you going to lie down at night when the snow falls and the grass disappears?' Just for a moment his grandfather's face became stubborn and angry like before the war, before he lay in the bomb crater and they came back for him, and then he said in a clear voice, 'In the same place.'

It will stop raining before they reach Barnaul.

The special train will arrive at midnight of the eighth day and Shadrin will lie under the old blanket for another seven hours waiting for the morning, silently fighting against his hunger pains, looking through the dirty glass at the dim lamps of the station and the high, dark arch of the unloading crane, pondering the fact that he has made the entire journey in vain.

They will start unloading the trucks in the morning and won't finish until the evening. They will assign them to villages. Shadrin will drive his truck to the parking lot and spend only one night with everyone else. The next day they will take him to the district hospital, where he will spend two days. They will take a blood sample, a urine sample, the same bacteriological samples they take from people working in a canteen, a photofluorograph, a sample of gastric juice; and then they will take him to Barnaul, check his passport, travel warrant and case history, the results of his blood analysis, urine analysis, bacteriological analysis, photofluorograph and gastric juice analysis. To be on the safe side they will take all the samples again, they will give him injections, look at him kindly, feed him tablets by hand as though he were a dog, feed him milk soup, raw eggs, porridge with milk, prepare him for an operation, watch over his sleep.

Five days later they will undress him, put him on a trolley, cover him with a clean white sheet and roll him into the large operating theatre with its harsh lighting like a banqueting hall, transfer him to the operating table, give him a general anaesthetic, cut him open, take a look, sew him up and wheel him back to the ward. They won't tell him anything, but he'll say, 'You can tell me, I don't give a damn.' Then they'll tell him, No drinking, no smoking, no spicy food, you can't do that with an ulcer, and so forth, and he will remember his grandfather lying on the burnt grass under the nut tree and say, 'That's not the problem.' He will lie in the hospital for another three weeks, the pain will go away and he will feel like he did forty years earlier when everyone that he knew was still alive. They will book him a plane ticket. Before he leaves he will ask the nurse for a pencil and a sheet of paper, she will bring them and he will sit beside his locker and at first draw something that looks like a fish with a tail but no fins, then draw in a pair of bulging eyes and long whiskers, and then a pair of big, outspread claws.

## 2

On the evening of the day when Shadrin left them and went to his truck, they ran out of vodka. They went to the conductor and the conductor said, 'No, I haven't got any.' But the next morning he was still drunk as a skunk as he staggered around the carriage with a sack and collected the empty bottles.

For a while they slouched aimlessly around the carriage with dehydrated brains and bellies, they spoke to each other and their furred tongues stuck to the back of their throats, and their eyes itched as though they'd been reading furiously for a long time.

Then they found a broom. They swept out the scraps of torn newspaper, apple cores, cucumber ends, spent matches, egg shells and ash, shards of glass, tin cans, fish skeletons and chicken bones from under the bunks; they washed all the frying pans, bowls, mugs, spoons, forks and knives and then, completely sober by now, they reversed the sheets on their beds, took off the pillow-cases and blanket covers, turned them inside out and put them back on that way. They felt an obsessive craving for cleanliness, they shaved and washed, cleaned their clothes and their shoes. Then they played cards, made conversation and drank warm, stale water.

When the special train reached its destination they were all asleep with the exception of Shadrin, who was lying on the seat of his truck under an old blanket riddled with holes and looking at the station lamps and the dark arch of the unloading crane.

Ratalov will be the first to get out of the carriage and set off, sinking up to his ankles in the dry white sand, towards the small lake a hundred metres from the railway embankment.

The flatcars with their trucks will be shunted under the crane and the carriage in which they travelled will be uncoupled. They will gather up their things, carry them out and pile them up under the concrete overhang of the station building.

Ratalov will be assigned to a group of six, along with Zhigan, Sharov, Bragin and the black cat.

They will drive their trucks to a small village two kilometres from the threshing floor.

They will be quartered in a new house without heating. They will each be given two mattresses and two blankets.

In the morning Shadrin will be taken off to hospital.

The black cat will leave them to start crossing people's paths.

They will be shown the mess hall, a dilapidated, crooked house smelling of offal, they will be invited inside, they will go in and see a triangular shard of a mirror on the wall, five large tables painted green and one small one, brightly coloured, fly-spotted curtains at the windows; in the corner at the little table they will see a short fingerless hermaphrodite, with wide female hips and grey stubble on his chin and a plate of pea soup on the table in front of him. Ratalov will remember him for a long time, sitting there at his small table in the corner, hating both men and women alike, eating his soup disdainfully with a spoon bent into the shape of a poker; he will remember the broken piece of a ruler fastened to his wrist with a tight elastic band and the way he stuck the handle of the spoon between the piece of ruler and his fingerless palm.

Then they will go to a shop where they sell beer in barrels.

A couple of days will go on fitting out their trucks. They will seal up the cracks in the walls of the backs of the trucks so the grain won't trickle out, and the carpenters will install wooden grilles for those of them who agree to drive cattle to slaughter.

Then it will start to rain. It will rain non-stop for a week and their travel warrants will be rendered useless by the impassable roads.

On the second day of rain a short red-haired woman with a coarse, weathered face will come to them in dirty rubber boots and a short yellow coat and bring a five-litre jar of beer. She will stand the jar on the windowsill and say in a husky voice, 'There you go. Help yourselves.' Then she will take off her coat and boots, impudently slip her little feet into Bragin's slippers, open the jar, cast an eye over lanky, skinny Ratalov, purse her pale, weathered lips, wink her painted eye at him and say, 'How about a drink, skeleton?'

Help-Yourselves will come to them every day, bring them beer, yell at them, call them weaklings, vilify the town where they live, throw everything at them that comes to hand. They will take her for a madwoman, but they won't say anything or throw her out, because when it's raining only a madman would turn away a woman and beer.

On the fourth day of rain Ratalov, drunk as a loon, will meet a large, imperturbable woman with an impassive sunburnt face, long black hair, a low, quiet voice and a dusky look in her eyes. He will never be able to remember how they met and how he ended up in her house; Zhigan will tell him he went out to relieve himself and didn't come back. Ratalov will wake up in a small, unfamiliar room under the dusky gaze of the imperturbable black-haired woman. Behind Ratalov's long, repulsive mug, broken nose, rotten teeth and crooked jaw, she will discern his true vocation: to do good. She will discern his childlike ability to believe in fairy-tales if they are told convincingly, an ability other women failed to destroy in him. She will feed him and brush her breasts across the back of his head as she clears the table, and her swarthy, seven-year-old son will hover around her, cunning and spiteful.

On the fifth day of rain Ratalov will gather up all his stuff and move in with her.

He will live with her for two months, during which time she will never once ask him for anything. Under her dusky gaze he will mend the fence bent crooked by the wind and rain and paint it blue, with never a thought about how the rain will wash off the paint and the wind will blow the fence down again. Obsessed by the urge to make things last for ever, obsessed by his hatred for self-annihilation and the erosion of life and premature corruption, imagining himself an artist from the time of the Renaissance, he will dispel the mirages of desolation by his very appearance, sawing down the old, worm-eaten pear tree and chopping enough firewood to last ten winters, building a new kennel for the moulting dog, who will throw himself at him in a movement too swift for the eye to catch, the electrified movement of a basilisk, but will be pulled up short by his chain. He will shore up the shed that was on the point of collapse, he will use the money from petrol he has sold and coal he has delivered to the neighbours to buy the child a few clothes, a set of games and some fluffy toys, he will stack up the shelves of the cellar with tinned goods, buy orange and blue tablecloths, buy a flower vase painted with dancing figures, quite sure in his mind that no matter how it all ends, these will be the best days of his life.

Occasionally he will run across Bragin and Zhigan and learn that Shadrin has had an operation and been sent home, and then he will forget, absorbed in his renaissance of the Renaissance, and only remember Shadrin once in two months as he lies on the narrow divan beside the sleeping black-haired woman under a picture showing a leopard hunting high in the mountains, at the moment when the night is about to course through his blood, plundering his very soul.

Afterwards, when Ratalov, born to do good, gets out of jail and realizes that peace and spiritual emptiness are the same thing, he will often remember Shadrin, born for prison and war, who exhausted his monstrous reserves of strength and anger in battle with himself and was struck down ignominiously by ulcers and cancer.

After his return to his former life, he will recall a great many other things.

They didn't speak to each other much; he mended, painted and reinforced things without saying a word, and she silently got undressed, gazing at him duskily, and got into bed with him.

He brought her coal and crushed stone, which he later mixed with cement and used to reinforce the doorstep. He brought her oats and wheat, while he worked in a grain elevator.

Afterwards, when the neighbours grew fed up with watching the imperturbable black-haired bitch get the things they had to buy for free and someone reported Ratalov, he got away with the coal and crushed stone, but the oats and wheat were regarded as embezzlement of state property, and the sale of the petrol as speculation in state property for personal gain.

They came for him one morning in late November, when they were due to leave in just three days, a stocky sergeant, a young lieutenant and a tall captain with a stoop in a uniform as crumpled as a bed-sheet, and first they came into the imperturbable black-haired woman's house and under her dusky gaze they discovered two hundred kilograms of wheat in four sacks and three sacks of oats. The captain with the stoop twitched his moustache and asked how much she'd paid; she said she hadn't paid anything and she said, 'I didn't know anything about it,' and she said, 'I didn't see anything.' The captain with the stoop asked, 'Did you ask him to bring the wheat?' She gave him a dusky look and said, 'I didn't ask him for anything.' 'So he hid the stolen wheat in your house in order to take it to Moscow later, to feed his chickens,' the captain with the stoop drawled. She said, 'I don't know.' The captain with the stoop asked, 'Where is he?' She looked at him duskily and said, 'I don't know.' 'Where's your uncle, boy?' the young lieutenant asked the black-haired woman's son, who was hovering around, cunning and spiteful. The boy said, 'In the . . .'

After that they drove to the house where the drivers lived, left their car out on the road and went inside. Apart from Zhigan, who was sitting on his bed sewing up his shirt, there was no one there. The captain with the stoop asked where Ratalov was and when he'd be back; Zhigan looked at them and said he didn't know any such person, there was no one by that name there. The captain with the stoop named the municipal registration number of Ratalov's truck and the number of his trailer. Zhigan said those weren't Moscow numbers, more likely Minsk or Magadan numbers, and he asked, 'What's up? Has he had an accident or knocked someone down?' The captain with the stoop said, 'No,' and he said to the others, 'Let's go.' They spotted Ratalov's truck outside the shop. Ratalov was standing in the queue and talking with Bragin. They went into the shop, called out the number of the truck and asked whose it was; Ratalov said, 'Mine,' and then he asked, 'Is it in the way?' The captain with the stoop said, 'No, it's okay.' They waited until Ratalov bought his bread and cigarettes.

Then they took him, and the crowd of local women waiting their turn to buy something and then eat it began cackling and came tumbling out of the shop after them, led by a fat, red sales assistant, who left her place at the counter to the peevish cleaning-woman, who was so furious and curious she was ready to explode like a ripe carbuncle.

'. . . Lord . . .'

'. . . God . . .'

'. . . my . . .'

'. . . that's . . .'

'. . . what he . . .'

'. . . deserves . . .'

'. . . the thief, all that wheat he . . .'

'. . . for her . . .'

'. . . and she . . .'

'Is he the one who stabbed his wife and two sons to death?' shouted a deaf old woman, clutching at the sales assistant's sleeve.

'No, he . . .'

'. . . mended, painted, stole gr . . .'

'. . . sold petrol, at twenty litres for six . . .'

'. . . bought some from him, did you?'

'. . . no I didn't, I'm an hon . . .'

'. . . the slut . . .'

'Is he the one who raped the little girls at the back of the graveyard?' shouted out the deaf old woman, tugging on the sales assistant's sleeve.

'No, no, granny, he sto . . .'

'. . . openly. I paid like everyone else, and he openly gave her . . .'

'. . . brought the bitch wheat and oa . . .'

'. . . got a hankering for . . .'

'. . . coal, crushed stone, oats, wheat . . .'

'. . . a vase for flowers and . . .'

'. . . me a truckload of coal for fifty . . .'

'. . . tablecloths, blue and oran . . .'

'. . . I ask him, give me some crushed stone to lay on the path to the vegetable garden, and he says, give me a tenn . . .'

'. . . clothes for the brat and fluffy anim . . .'

'Is he the one who hammered a pinewood stake into his sister's belly?' shouted out the deaf old woman, tugging on the sales assistant's sleeve.

'. . . Lord . . .'

'. . . and . . .'

'. . . in the rain . . .'

'. . . and . . .'

'. . . not in the rain . . .'

'. . . he did . . .'

'. . . us . . .'

'. . . bastards . . .'

'. . . bastards . . .'

'Officer, officer,' shouted out the deaf old woman, who confused day and night, money and newspapers, men and women in the cobweb of old age, 'check to see if he hasn't got a pistol or a knife. Hasn't he got a knife?'

The tall captain with the stoop barked out, 'Enough.'

Ratalov closed his eyes, then opened them again, expecting to see ruined houses, burned villages, charred earth and smoke, but all he saw was a crowd of people and Bragin, who was standing at one side without moving.

They will take Ratalov away to Biisk.

## 3

The special train reached its destination at midnight of the eighth day.

At the same time as Shadrin was lying on the seat of his truck under an old blanket riddled with holes and looking at the station lamps and the dark arch of the unloading crane, Bragin was asleep on an upper bunk in the passenger carriage.

They woke Bragin at seven o'clock in the morning. He got up and gathered his things together without hurrying. Then he looked out of the window and saw Ratalov, who was sinking up to his ankles in the dry, white sand as he walked towards the small lake a hundred metres from the railway embankment.

The flatcars carrying the trucks were shunted under the crane and the carriage in which they travelled was uncoupled. They took out their things and piled them up under the concrete overhang of the station building.

Bragin was assigned to a group of six together with Zhigan, Shadrin and Ratalov.

They drove their trucks to a small village two kilometres from the threshing floor.

They were quartered in a new house.

The next morning Shadrin was taken away to hospital.

They were shown the mess room, a decrepit, crooked house reeking of offal; they were invited in. They went in and saw a triangular shard of a mirror on the wall, five large tables painted green and one small one, brightly coloured curtains at the windows; in the corner at the small table they saw a short hermaphrodite with no fingers, with broad woman's hips and grey stubble on his chin.

A couple of days went on fitting out the trucks.

Then it began to rain.

On the second day of rain a redheaded woman with a coarse, weathered face came to them in dirty rubber boots and a short, yellow coat, and brought them a five-litre jar of beer. She put the jar on the windowsill and said in a husky voice, 'There you go. Help yourselves.'

On the fourth day of rain Ratalov, drunk as a loon, went outside to relieve himself and didn't come back till the next morning.

On the fifth day of rain Ratalov gathered up his stuff and left them.

Help-Yourselves came to them every day; she brought beer, yelled, called them weaklings, got drunk, vilified the town where they lived, threw everything that came to hand at them. They took her for a madwoman, but they didn't say anything and they didn't throw her out.

Help-Yourselves invited them round to her place, but they didn't go.

When it stopped raining and dried out a bit, Zhigan made his first run. He filled the tanks of his trailer up to the brim and went to Kamen-on-the-Ob for condoms.

Then he went to her.

During the next week the others went to see her too.

The last but one to go to her was Dyukin, who was almost sixty. Before he went Zhigan looked at him and said, 'Try not to disappoint the poor girl.' Dyukin soon came back and said he wouldn't go to her again. Zhigan asked, 'Why?' Dyukin said, 'There's a smell of death in her bed.' Zhigan laughed and said, 'There's the same smell in every bed. It's life smelling of death.'

Bragin was the last to go to her.

Two months later, when he is taking his truck to be loaded up for Moscow, Bragin will run off the road at speed, blinded by the headlights of an oncoming refrigerated truck, and overturn his trailer into the Kuludinsk canal. He will clamber out, soaked through, on to the road and as he wipes the blood from his broken face, he will remember Help-Yourselves.

Bragin arrived at her place; without turning on the light, she took him through to a small, dark bedroom.

She opened the curtains on the window, and the moonlight came streaming into the bedroom.

She went up to him.

Bragin looked at the woman's coarse, weathered face with wrinkles around the eyes, like the face of a tired lumberjack.

She undressed slowly, and he saw her young, supple body.

It wasn't her.

It was her.

She lay down.

Now she will say: Come to me.

She said, 'Come to me.'

Bragin undressed and lay down.

Her face changed instantly; it became childlike and expressive, even in the moonlight, which turns the living into the dead.

Her cold woman's hands touched Bragin.

Now she will say: I couldn't give a damn about all the others, I was waiting just for you. Don't ever go away.

She said, 'I couldn't give a damn about all the others, I was waiting just for you. Don't ever go away.' She looked at him helplessly, tenderly, swallowing her tears.

Bragin kissed her, staring at the pillow.

Now she will ask: Do you love me?

She asked, 'Do you love me?' and looked at him imploringly.

Bragin said, 'Yes. I love you.'

Now she will ask: Very much?

She asked, 'Very much?'

Bragin said, 'Very much.'

Very, very much?

Very, very much.

Now she will ask: You won't leave me, will you?

She asked, 'You won't leave me, will you? You won't leave me?' And she looked at him through eyes filled with tears, a perfect picture of the sincerity of a nun, the innocence of an embryo.

They were a single stratum of the earth.

That's all.

And then she stretched lazily, turned towards him, twisted her pale, weathered lips into a mocking grin and said, 'Good.'

# Armed Defence

The first thing he did was burn all the books, paintings, reproductions and photographs, believing they might distract and confuse him if they caught his eye or simply get in his way when it came to the siege. It took him the whole day, not because there were a lot of them, but because they burned slowly. The leather bindings of the books and the gilded frames of the pictures reduced him to despair. He stood motionless in front of the fireplace in his long brown dressing-gown and tattered slippers, thinking there was not enough time, not enough time, watching the flames choke on the leather bindings of the old folios like a dog unable to swallow a bone stuck in its throat. The fire shunned the gilded frames like water and he suspected they weren't wood at all, or they were wood, but coated with a thick layer of old, rock-hard putty. The pictures themselves had burned away long ago. At last the leather bindings crumbled into ash and the gilded frames, untouched by the fire, burst into flame under his frenzied gaze, and then he collapsed exhausted into an armchair and felt he had fallen from an unimaginable height, as if a god had fallen to earth; he felt heavy and too deadly tired to do everything that had to be done.

When his strength returned there was a thunderstorm outside. He went out on to the terrace, looked towards the forest and thought if they came at him now it would be all over and he needn't have burned anything.

He tried not to think about that.

And he thought that if they sent cannon, tanks and motorized guns against him in order to level to the earth everything that since time immemorial had been equal to the earth, he would be powerless to do anything. This reduced him to a despair deeper than he had felt when the leather bindings and gilded frames would not burn in the fire.

He tried not to think about that.

And then he thought they could mobilize aircraft that would annihilate him and annihilate everything that was not him for a thousand miles around.

But he said, 'No, they won't send tanks and they won't mobilize aircraft. That's the same as launching a battle-ready nuclear warship just to chop up a single jelly-fish with its propellers.'

He tried not to think about that.

He went into the bedroom, opened the wardrobe, took out an old military uniform and a camouflage cloak that only camouflaged on grass in patchy sunshine. He found a clothes-brush under the bed, wetted it and painstakingly cleaned the uniform and the heavy, riveted boots. He got undressed and took a cold shower. Then he put on the uniform and the boots, and the weight of them pinioned his feet to the floor; and he donned the camouflage cloak over the uniform and felt like a tree that had to walk. Little by little he grew used to walking in the boots and used to ignoring his own sluggishness, believing the tortoise owed its longevity to its very sluggishness. He thought he had to think just as slowly as he moved, otherwise he would die on the inside much sooner than on the outside. And in addition he had to slow the coursing of the blood in his veins, that way there would be less wear and tear, because the friction would not be so strong; slow the rhythm of his heartbeats, because a hammer used to knock in a thousand nails will wear out sooner than a hammer used to knock in one; check the impetuous torrent of his thoughts to the sluggish rhythm of a clock's pendulum, that was the secret.

He fell asleep in the armchair long after midnight and woke at midday with the thought of tanks and aircraft. He noticed the thought of tanks and aircraft made his arms and legs tremble, his hair fall out, his vision grow dim and his mind grow numb. And he realized if he thought about tanks and aircraft all the time he would live no longer than a butterfly. And then he thought he must have already fallen into their hands a long time ago. He listened and gave a deep sigh. It was quiet. And then he remembered about silent murder, and he forsook food and water, because it might all be poisoned and he realized in the end he would have to forsake sleep, because in his sleep a man is as helpless as a thing.

He tried not to think about that.

He went down to the first floor and checked that the locks and bolts on the front door were closed. Once he was certain they couldn't gain silent entry to the house that way he checked the bolts on the shutters of all the windows on the first and second floors.

And then he thought about the terrace that stretched out towards the forest. Deep down he knew for sure they would come from the forest and first they would try to take the wide open terrace. Now he realized he had always known this, even when he was born blind, deaf and dumb he had known for sure they would come from the forest and first they would try to take the wide open terrace.

He set up two heavy machine-guns on the terrace and it took him half the day just to drag them out there. He made them fast, screwing the welded steel base-plates to the surface of the terrace with immense bolts like the ones that hold high-voltage pylons steady, so that the machine-guns would not be turned against him if the terrace was taken anyway. In case the terrace was taken he set up a light machine-gun in the room facing it, its drum loaded with fragmentation bullets with cross-shaped notches on their hollow heads. He set up light machine-guns in every room and released the safety catches because there might not be time for that later.

And again he thought about aircraft and tanks and his mind was numbed by despair.

But he said, 'No, they won't send tanks and they won't mobilize aircraft. That's the same as launching a battle-ready nuclear warship just to chop up a single jelly-fish with its propellers.'

He stood on the terrace facing the forest between the heavy machine-guns with their mountings secured to the right and the left by steel pins allowing the barrels a thirty-degree arc of swing. He thought if they advanced on the terrace in wedge formation, he would secure the heavy machine-gun on the left with its barrel turned to the extreme right and brace a piece of steel against the trigger, then take up his own position behind the heavy machine-gun on the right because it was closer to the door into the room facing on to the terrace, the one he would retreat into. That way he would counter the enemy's wedge with a cone of machine-gun fire from two points, drive a wedge into the wedge. But while the outer edges of the wedge of machine-gun fire were effective, the inside was hollow. And then he paced out the distance from one heavy machine-gun to the other, calculated the arc of swing of the barrels and calculated the distance to the point where the lines of machine-gun fire would intersect, forming the cone. And then he took an axe, climbed down from the terrace on to the ground and paced out the distance he had calculated to that point and cut a large notch in the trunk of a tree, and that was the point where the lines of machine-gun fire would intersect.

If the enemy's wedge penetrated the hollow space of the cone which was not raked by the heavy machine-gun fire, both machine-guns became useless and he would be forced to retreat into the room next to the terrace, stand at the light machine-gun with the fragmentation bullets and fire through the doors leading on to the terrace, over the parapet. In that case the light machine-gun mounted in the room would be more important than the two heavy machine-guns mounted on the terrace, which were only intended to bring down as many men as he could manage before they broke through past the tree marked with the notch.

But he said, 'They won't advance in wedge formation.'

If they attacked in a phalanx, in close order, and went on to surround the house, one of the heavy machine-guns, the one on the left in fact, without a gunner, with its barrel secured in position, became almost useless, since its bullets were easy to dodge. And if they put off taking the terrace for a while, he could expect the assault to come from the direction of the front door after they surrounded the house, but he couldn't abandon the terrace either.

He tried not to think about that and not to think about the hunger and thirst, knowing perfectly well it would be stupid to poison himself now when everything he wanted to do was done and all he needed to do was to wait.

He walked through the rooms once again, checked the machine-guns and kissed the barrel of each one, and he kissed the knife which he always carried, with the blade that rang like crystal.

Using ash from the fireplace he drew arrows on the walls of the rooms, having first worked out and clarified for himself his line of retreat from room to room, and he thought this would be the actual route if he conducted his defence of the house starting from the terrace. But in addition he drew continuous arrows on the walls of the rooms for the line of retreat he had to follow if they attacked from the direction of the front door and he had to begin his retreat from the entrance hall. Both sets of arrows converged in the most remote corner room, where there was no furniture and no machine-guns, where many years ago he had been born.

# The Surveyor

He settled his accounts with them at the end of the day, counting up the number of dead flies in the house with painstaking care, and paying a kopeck for each one; they didn't clean them off the walls and doors and windows until the tally had been completed, and then they brought the old rusty food tins for him to make an equally painstaking tally of the Colorado beetles collected from the potato plants, and after arming himself with a thin twig he would lean his thin, austere face down over the tins, pressing his pale lips together as he fixed the wriggling mass of insects with his stare and counted them just as painstakingly, breaking into a cold sweat every time the unfailing intuition nurtured by three wars whispered that he had counted the same beetle twice, because while he only paid a kopeck for each fly that was killed, he paid two for each beetle, so he couldn't afford to make a mistake. After that they doused the beetles with petrol and squatted down on their haunches to set them alight, peering into the flickering tongues of flame and the black smoke, while he stood off to one side under the tall pear-tree, in the spot where they usually buried the cat's litters of blind kittens, leaning on his thick, smooth stick and pretending to be gazing in the direction of the swamp, but actually keeping a close eye on them to make sure the beetles were all burned to the very last one because he thought: Tomorrow they could stick the same beetles they caught today under my nose again, not in order to get rich, of course, but just in order to vex me; and then he thought: To take revenge for my honesty.

But his unrelenting venomous resentment, his primordial craving for unbounded tyrannical dominion in the sovereign state of his own family, prevailing over the craving for material well-being, prevailing over the craving of his blood for glory and the craving of his mind for solitude, together with his savage, ferocious methods of quashing the slightest ripple of insubordination, effectively excluded the possibility of lies even being conceived in his presence. Neither his older nor his younger grandson would ever have dared to lie to him, for the very thought of attempting to match wits with him in cunning and then being caught out in a lie, as seemed to them inevitable, filled their hearts with a leaden, enervating terror and shackled their tongues with an inflexible honesty, making them feel as though their mouths were filled with cold, sour aluminium wire that had sprouted from the swollen tonsils of respect and hate. Even if he hadn't counted the dead flies and captured beetles, they would not have been able to deceive him, just as they could not deceive their own minds, which kept a steady, impartial account of what their hands did, and even if he were at the far end of the world, whatever they might do for the kopecks he paid them would still have taken place under his omnipresent gaze, and the eyes which always followed them everywhere, as though they had grown into the orbits in their own skulls, appeared to be watching them from the cracks in the fence or from behind the cross on the icon-frame, although they knew that at that moment he was on his way to the bread shop or hunting wild duck in the tall swamp grass: they saw his eyes watching them through the dense foliage of the orchard three metres above the stunted yellow flowers as they secured a haystack with long, stout poles so that it wouldn't be scattered by the wind, when meanwhile he was roaming the meadows in search of his lost wristwatch; and another time they could have sworn they saw the toe of his boot peeping out under the door of the privy, when they were absolutely certain that he was in the pine forest, collecting the cones their grandmother wanted.

He had eleven children, two sons and nine stunningly beautiful daughters, and there was talk that he had an illegitimate son in Kiev, although no one knew for certain. The first two daughters, Maria and Olga, had reason to remember the war much better than the rest of his children, because they were older; and apart from that, both of them were the right age to be among the women whom the Germans had herded off to their own country. But while the first had managed to avoid that fate by following the advice of her girlfriends and gorging herself on horse-manure just before the next group was due to be dispatched to the military train, after which she lay at death's door for three days and three nights in the cool silent twilight of her parents' house, the second had been picked up before she could make a run for it and delivered in a German lorry to the huge, dusty troop-train, in which she arrived in Germany six days later, one of many eighteen-year-old girls who would never recover from their fright. She lived in Germany for seven months and four days, until that night bombing raid when her right leg was torn off by a fragment of shrapnel that went on to shatter her left one, after which she was promptly dispatched back to Russia, since now she was incapacitated and when she recovered she could never be such an efficient dishwasher as all the others. At home, when the straitjacket of pain had become an integral part of her world, of her waking and sleeping life, she developed gangrene and her right leg, which had been sawn off in Germany, was shortened by another ten centimetres in Kharkov, where she lay for four months in a dirty military hospital, smelling of a foreign country and waiting for death, feeling time burning away as quickly as a Bickford fuse, living over and over again the piercing, blinding pain of that moment which for her had irrevocably usurped the place of childbirth, when the bomb fragment had shredded the fragile fabric of her life. After she came home from the hospital for a long time the walls of the house became the boundaries of her existence and she was afraid to cross them even in her thoughts, so that her dreams became cramped and almost real, for with only rare exceptions the action in them took place within those same boundaries, and even when awake she never set herself the goal of surmounting them. Meanwhile Krainov went on having children and the gap between their births was never more than three years. It was these children, her sister and brothers, and his children's children, who later deprived Olga of her name, unerringly discerning in her face and her eyes that they and they alone had infused meaning into the cramped space of her life and given her back her elemental purpose, or perhaps even something greater, so that eventually she became Mother of All Children.

But not all of them survived to the mid-fifties. The sixth daughter died when she had barely opened her dark-blue eyes to glimpse the absurd, inverted world through which the barren shades of her parents, brothers and sisters glided: her name was given to a rough-hewn rock one-quarter-buried in the ground above a grave. After that first Klavdiya and then Alexandra died of tuberculosis, the two girls reputed to be the greatest beauties of the village: but when the Mother of All Children said that their father's most beautiful daughter was the one whose name had been given to the rock, no one chose to argue with her.

Krainov himself took the deaths of his children harder than anyone else, because in addition to suffering, his grief also contained a wayward rebelliousness that craved expression, that was nourished by the certain knowledge that he had more right to his children than some stupid death which had done absolutely nothing to help bring them into the world. Sitting on the chair under the old carved wooden clock which had once been an object of pride to him, with his entire body twitching as he tried to suppress his hiccups, he sucked in hatred on ancient, rock-hard fruit drops, his head lowered and his blazing eyes scorching through the floorboards, thrusting his furiously concentrated gaze deep into the earth like some long, incandescent metal shaft that served simultaneously as a weapon and an echo sounder, striving in vain to reach down to the roaring fires in the bowels of the earth and summon forth an effusion of hell. For the only thing that he saw in his children was the most important thing of all to him, the augmentation of his own flesh, the extension of the world of his own ego. Their every movement had to be realized only through the single, indivisible brain that was housed in the vault of his skull, and in his deluded frenzy, in his frenzied faith in the indivisibility of the unitary organism of the family, he exploded at the slightest manifestation of intelligence or independence from those he had created, because his numerous children were merely the result of his desire to expand himself and dominate some greater whole. That was why the death of three of his children reduced him to furious despair, because in dying they had determined the fate of their bodies independently, isolated within them as though inside some protective capsule, and even before they died they were already remote from him and free of his importunate claims. For many years they appeared in his dreams in the form of sad, slow fishes behind the thick, transparent glass walls of a gigantic aquarium, where they swam sluggishly and aimlessly through the mysterious dark-green water, among the artificially cultivated waterweed and the little brown snails, out of reach of the sound of his voice as it lashed against the glass and the frenzied heat of his frantic commands to rejoin the army of his children. After these dreams he liked to say that in their illnesses and their deaths people were like fish, but no one understood.

And so he had lost three children. But their deaths were only the beginning of the losses which he had been anticipating and expecting for a long time since he had recollected one night that he himself was lost to people and forgotten by them: as his children grew up, he realized that the unitary organism of the family was hopelessly small and frail in comparison with the size and power of the outside world for which they left him when they set up their own families and dissolved into their newly invented freedom, although they never entirely lost contact with him and always settled in the immediate neighbourhood, which flattered his vanity, since he thought they were demonstrating a lack of confidence in their own strength and a desire to have him there to protect them in case of sudden need. They did not maintain close contact with him, though, evidently wary of inescapable enslavement, but their little children often visited his house to deliver sweets and lemonade to the Mother of All Children and they kissed their grandmother and stared into his eyes attentively and suspiciously as they stood in front of him, waiting for a word of censure or a word of approval, unaware that their parents had shattered something in his life, that they had destroyed the system which he had built up for his family without the slightest notion of differentiation, without his book-keeper's mind acknowledging in the slightest degree the multifaceted wisdom of nature.

He sent his last two daughters, Evgeniya and Margarita, off to the city when the youngest was barely fifteen years old, for that was when he had finally become convinced that the time of sym-biotic relations within the family was irrevocably past and gone and his conceptual structures, in which he always assigned him-self the role of the load-bearing element, were as unstable as human thought itself. The two daughters left on the same day, and so the following day they were already in the city under the liberal supervision of his cousin, a stout peroxide blonde with a heavy square jaw and ears as small as leaves of clover, who had actually been the one who suggested he should send his daugh-ters to the city. She was the one who helped Evgeniya to get a job in a canteen as an assistant cook and she found Margarita work as a nanny in a kindergarten, where the girl only worked for a very short time until she reached sixteen and gave in her notice, then once again with the help of her father's cousin she got a job as a waitress in a decrepit restaurant, and six months later she married a short, balding twenty-five-year-old man, a former miner who was now the warden in the female hall of residence where Margarita lived as the youngest of four girls sharing a single room. He used to come to their room every day, shabby and untidy, with his plain face unshaven and his eyes ravaged by frequent lengthy bouts of drinking: he smelled of the strong tobacco of cheap *papyroses* and the thick, sweet fumes of drink. He would sit down on a chair and immediately light up, put the matches away in the pocket of his threadbare velveteen jacket and cross his legs, presenting to the public gaze a large, tattered and unpolished shoe that was enough to horrify any woman, and once he was comfortably settled to his own satisfaction, he would begin talking the most unimaginable nonsense, in which bragging was followed by semi-drunken ravings and the semi-drunken ravings were followed by more bragging. In short, the sight of this man could hardly have inspired the most fevered imagination to believe that he carried considerable intellectual potential hidden away inside his head, as though it was concealed by the darkness of night, but nonetheless that was the case, for not only did he carry off Krainov's youngest daughter and the son they had together to Moscow, he also travelled all over the world and achieved outstanding success in the epistolary genre of literature, which allowed them to live in relative comfort and contentment.

Left alone with his wife and the one-legged Mother of All Children, Krainov felt like an official who had been unjustly demoted. Never having aspired to an understanding of the processes of life, devoid of objective insight, wounded but by no means defeated, he set about restoring his own dignity. Displaying his arrogance and disdain, constantly unleashing on them his inexhaustible reserves of ungovernable wrath, he would sometimes fall silent, but only in order to exploit the brief silence to elicit some insignificant action or look they gave him which might cause insult or offence. Sometimes, camouflaging himself behind some illness, he would lie on the divan, filling the room with his heavy sighs and heart-rending groans, his angry eyes half-closed as they constantly followed the women's movements, straining to see whether they exhibited any signs of gladness or gloating over his serious physical condition, and whether they were as sincere in their concern and their professions of sympathy as they tried to appear.

Meanwhile his withdrawal from other people had begun, a gradual, almost imperceptible but inevitable withdrawal into old age, into the world where those who are rich in the past but poor in the future grow to resemble unneeded naturalistic portraits. When he entered this world, however, he was still filled with the explosive fumes of pride, tangled in a web of contradictory desires and instincts; still strong in body and spirit, he retrieved thoughts that had crept away from him and returned them to the nest of his brain with the lightning-swift gesture of a snake-catcher, resolutely determined to retain control over his magnificent memory to the very end of his days. As he was transformed into an introverted personality, drawing his strength and certainty from within himself, he began to care for his own appearance with a punctiliousness untypical of old age, shaving his neck and cheeks every day, trimming his handsome grey beard and his narrow, well-tended moustache. When he took his place at the table in the morning to drink his mug of tea and eat his invariable lump of butter swimming in water in an aluminium bowl, his carefully combed grey hair smelled of eau-de-cologne and his bright gleaming boots gave off a fresh smell of shoe-polish.

He had never actually been a hermit, but he had led a relatively isolated life. Where formerly he had associated with other people quite widely and quite often, working as a cattle procurement officer, buying up cows, pigs and sheep from local people, haggling over deals and quite often getting involved in protracted squabbles, when he became a land surveyor he was already exceptionally taciturn, with an extremely orthodox approach to his work and a ferocious geriatric honesty. However, all of these praiseworthy qualities disappeared without trace the moment he was back among his family, in the enclosed space of his tiny imaginary kingdom where everything, even the dust, obeyed only him, where dissimulation and greed took possession of his mind with the same speed as white spirit invades a small rag, and mutiny by its inhabitants would have seemed more absurd than mutiny by its objects. Here he ruled his wife, who was finding it more and more difficult to move around, and his one-legged daughter with the painstaking precision of an animated cartoon artist, whose work he had regarded as the height of patient effort ever since the time one of his grandsons who came to spend the holidays with them had explained to him how it was possible to draw figures so as to show them running. Here he ruled, basing his methods on the outstanding achievements of state intrigue and doggedly imitating the example of the great scoundrels, by means of deceitful slander, setting mother and one-legged daughter against each other the moment he noticed the slightest glimmer of tenderness between them, for in his opinion tenderness could lead to their becoming united. He always chose the right time to defame one of his sons, and always the very one who, by offering help, might have unforgivably improved his own standing in the eyes of his mother and in doing so humiliated and overshadowed him. He uncompromisingly swept aside any advice from outsiders, quite deaf to the influence of the outside world, believing that there was no one who had mastered the science of ruling better than he had and that there were no discoveries left to make in this area, for every possible experiment had already been carried out. He protected his domain with the vigilance of a man under siege, making himself equally inaccessible to his own children (he made an exception for his grandsons, attempting, not entirely without success, to make them his allies) and to people on the outside, whose malicious tongues were capable of generating endless rumours and damaging his reputation, although he had long ago told himself that a reputation was not something to be despised, but if it had already been damaged, then to hell with it. Rumours reached him that his sons, not wishing to leave the grandmother and Mother of All Children all winter without any coal, and knowing that he wouldn't do anything about it himself, were squabbling shamelessly among themselves about which of them should deliver the coal, no longer willing to draw a card or toss a coin as they used to do. For they remembered very clearly the last time they had come, when they had stood in front of him and asked him to allow them to build a water pump in the yard, because it was hard for the Mother of All Children to go the well on her one leg even with an empty bucket, let alone to come back with a full one. He had refused them on the spot, on the grounds that it would have meant digging up the entire yard and the garden as well. From all the things he told them so contemptuously, gazing at them with eyes full of cruel curiosity, attempting to sting them, to hurt them as badly as possible, they had realized that he wouldn't mind at all having a water pump, if they simply set it down in the centre of the yard and it started working; but as for all those underground pipes for the water-supply, they were quite out of the question. Then one of his sons had said to him, 'We could lay the pipes above ground,' and he had replied mockingly, 'O yes, so I could trip over them.' But there had been another reason, which he hoped had remained a secret from his children; he was forced to admit to himself that his refusal also sprang from the fact that they had been the first to suggest something he himself should have done a long time ago. He had also heard that in the village they were saying he owed money to his children, to each and every one of them, money he had borrowed a very long time ago, before they completely broke off relations. He said to the grandmother, 'Have you heard what they're saying?' and he said, 'Seems I owe those sons of bitches money!' The grandmother said to him, 'But it's true, father,' and she said, 'That's the way things are'; and he smiled grimly under his handsome, regular grey moustache and said, 'Natter, bloody natter,' and then with sudden fury he said,

'If I decide to make them pay back their debt to me, they'll have to give me back their crappy little lives!' And he said, 'Hides, giblets and all.' But to himself he thought: What a fucking pain, eh? and he thought: I'd like to know how a tree can be in debt to some crappy little branch that's dropped off it, or to its own shitty fallen leaves!

The process of accumulating material wealth had long ceased to interest Krainov. Not only did he not buy anything for the house, he spent nothing on clothes either, calculating that he had more than enough clothes and shoes to last until he died. When the grandmother attempted to object he told her rudely, 'Shut your mouth!' and he said, 'We've even got a television!' And he devoted all his love, tenderness and jealousy without remainder to paper roubles, barely even tolerating material property, using it disdainfully, in the knowledge that it was not possible to live without beds, tables and chairs, but not constantly counting his objects or planning to increase their number, unlike his money, because in his opinion he already had the most important things. He had a smooth-barrelled shotgun, the sight of which roused him to a fury once every year, on the day when he had to pay a tax of fifteen roubles for it; he had a crystal receiver tuned to a forbidden wavelength and in the evenings he would submerge himself in its hissing sound and listen to various kinds of singing; he had a greasy old divan which had once soaked up the blood of childbirth and on which, when he stretched out at full length, he felt perfectly at peace, because under the carefully slit upholstery he kept his three per cent state loan bonds and no one could filch them because he was lying on them. He had a cracked sideboard painted pharmacy-white and in its big drawers and little drawers he hid the oat biscuits confiscated many years ago from the Mother of All Children, like round pieces of pumice, good for nothing except

perhaps for scraping ingrained fuel oil off the palms of your
hands, and the yellow caramels he had also confiscated, which
over the years had turned from confectionery into ceramics, and
a few bottles of last year's sour, fermented lemonade; these were
the sacrificial savings confiscated from the Mother of All
Children and destined for her if he and grandmother were to die
on the same day and there was nothing to eat or drink. He used
to say, as he took away her presents before the person who had
given them was barely out of the door, 'You'll be grateful to me
then!' and he used to think, 'What the hell does she need sweets
and biscuits for now, when I'm still alive and I can feed her?' The
same sideboard held the expensive fancy vodka glasses, empty
cans of imported beer sent from Moscow from time to time by
the husband of his second-last daughter, whose son had
explained to him how it was possible to draw figures to show
them running, and the labels with pictures of women's faces
torn from the plastic jars of Finnish processed cheese, which
served as Christmas tree decorations. And there was a corner of
the room that smelt of decay, and they guessed that was the
corner where he hid the money he had saved up, for that corner
had been declared the holy icon corner many years ago and it
was a long time since anyone had swept the floor there, or
removed the cobweb from the ceiling or attempted to whitewash the yellowed wall out of fear of igniting the furious blaze of
prohibition in his eyes. But the relative calm he felt during the
daylight hours concerning the money he had saved up would
often abandon him at night, when he would be woken by bright
warning flashes and leap from his bed with a face that glowed in
the darkness, and in a single elastic bound unimaginable at the
age of seventy, leap up on to the chair standing by the wall, tear
his shotgun off the wall together with its nail and a lump of plaster, and turn to face the corner, shattering the dark silence of the

house with a voice shuddering in fury as he yelled, 'Get away
from there! Get away from there, you bastard! I'll kill you, you
swine! I'll kill you, I say!' And he would carry on yelling until
the grandmother switched on the light and then, when he was
convinced that there was no one in the holy corner, he would
morosely hammer back in the nail that the strap of his shotgun
had pulled out, hang the gun on the wall and go to bed without
saying a word.

These nocturnal outbursts of fury usually came unpredictably,
but they occurred once a year with implacable regularity on the
night before the twenty-eighth of September, because that was
the day when they came from the district administrative centre
to fleece him of his annual membership fee for the hunters' association and he stood there in front of them, grey from lack of
sleep, clutching five roubles in his calloused fist, tormented by
the single question that he asked them every year, and they
imperturbably explained to him that it was to support the officials of the district, region and all-union associations, and to . . .
then he would say, 'Let them go rot, the bastards'; they would
explain it was for propaganda work, for publishing the magazine
*The Hunter* . . . then he would fix them with a malevolent stare
and say, 'I've never seen this magazine of yours,' and say, 'What
the hell use is it to me?' . . . and then say, 'That means they
should bring it to me for free, so why don't they bring it?' They
would tell him a subscription was extra and then he would yell,
'But I pay you, you bastards, every year I pay you!'; they would
say, 'But you don't pay'; he would say, 'Then what the hell do you
come round here bothering me for?' and they would say, 'To
confiscate your gun'; then he would say, 'You can go whistle for
my gun,' and he would say, 'There's your blasted fiver, I hope it
chokes you,' and he would say, 'You probably don't pay it yourselves'; then they would stick their membership cards under his

nose without saying a word and go away, and he would yell after them, asking how much the officials earned, screw the lot of them . . . and he would yell, 'Hey you, stop! Just how much do they get?'

He had already turned seventy-four when the twenty-year redemption term expired on his nineteen-sixty-two three per cent loan bonds, and every day that year from the first of January to the thirty-first of December he got up at four in the morning (although he normally got up at six o'clock in summer and seven o'clock in winter) and only ate early in the morning before they brought the newspapers, then sat by the window that looked out into the street, waiting for the newspapers to come, and from the moment he spotted the postman he followed him as he approached, half-rising from his chair, peeping out cautiously from behind the threadbare curtain, rubbing his cracked lips together impatiently, ready at any moment to draw back from the window if the postman so much as turned his head in his direction, and then, when he was quite sure that the postman had gone by, he crept stealthily out of the house, ignoring the grandmother, stepping soundlessly over the snow in his tattered slippers, opened the garden gate, alert and vigilant as a murderer, thrust his hands into the letter-box that was nailed to the outside of the fence, took out the newspaper and with undiminished caution, trying not to make the slightest sound that might betray his furious impatience, closed the gate, and then dashed headlong into the house, leaving damp tracks on the floor, sat on his bed, put on his spectacles and read the newspaper from cover to cover, endowing the printed letters with a meaning so great, so mighty and significant, that when he had read everything and not come across a single reference to the official redemption rates of the loan, he would sit there motionless for hours on end, enveloped in swirling clouds of fine, cold ash and debris, absorbed in the spectral catastrophe of the collapse of the vast edifice of Justice which he had been constructing since four o'clock in the morning, using ephemeral particles of scorched sand instead of stones and concrete slabs, and the following day everything was repeated all over again in precisely the same primordial sequence. And then at the end of the year, when he had still not discovered any table of redemption rates in the newspapers, he suddenly discovered within himself a stubborn, unshakeable faith in the state, in the Soviet Union, although his disbelief in the individual remained inviolate, because he was firmly convinced that a man alone was bound to lie and make excuses for himself, but society could not lie; he thought that telling lies was far harder for two people than for one, and he thought that for three people it was quite impossible, and then, true to his habit of turning everything on its head, he thought: After all, it wasn't just one son of a bitch who promised to pay us money on these blasted bonds after twenty years, they all promised, all of them together. Every day he read the extracts from the encyclopedic dictionary that he'd copied a long time ago into a thick exercise book yellowed with age, where he used to record the names and the parcels of land concerning which he had resolved disputes with the help of his measuring rod, and the recipes for medicinal teas, and the names of wild herbs, and where he had also written the following: 'A loan in civil law is a contract under the terms of which one party (the lender) grants the other (the borrower) the right of ownership to money or other items classified according to number, weight and measure (as of grain) and the borrower undertakes to return the same sum of money or an equal number of items of the same kind and quality,' and also he had written the following: 'A loan bond (from the verb "to bind") is a form of security payable to the bearer which gives the owner the right to receive an annual income in the form of a fixed percentage (or of dividends or coupon payments). Bonds are subject to redemption during a period of time specified at the time of issue of the loan.'

On the third of January the following year he set out to the district administrative centre through the deep, fresh, blue-shimmering snow and returned empty-handed because at the savings bank they told him what he already knew, that without the official table of loan redemption rates they couldn't pay out any money. He asked when the money would be paid out, because he needed a new definite date so that he could set himself the goal of living to see it, new promises not just from one person but from a thousand, which would allow him to believe, which would tell him: 'There, just stay alive till such and such a date and you'll get your money,' and then he would stay alive until that date no matter what; but they said to him, 'Nobody knows'; he asked, 'When will it be?'; they said to him, 'Are you deaf, or what?' and they said, 'We don't know'; then he asked, 'But what if I die?'; they told him, 'Your children will get it,' and they said, 'These bonds are payable to the bearer'; then he gazed at them for a while without speaking and jabbed himself in the chest with a finger and stood there as brown and unbending as a tree root, as he said, 'I have to get it, because I know what to do with it, and they know damn all,' and he said, 'They're the same kind of silly little girls as you are, and they'll get damn all from me! Can you understand that?' But they couldn't tell him anything. And on the way home, as his feet sank deep into the fresh snow, confounded and amazed at the pointlessness of his aspirations, his movements, his words, the pointlessness of his patience, he thought: God almighty! and he clenched his teeth and thought: God almighty! remembering how fifteen years ago he'd chased after grandmother, clutching a folded bicycle tyre tight in his fist, trying to catch her and beat her because when she wanted to shake out his mattress she had accidentally tipped the bonds out on to the floor and stepped on them; and he thought: God almighty! God almighty! when he recalled how he had tormented the nurses who used to come to give him injections and told him, 'You need to go to hospital,' and, 'You'll peg it at home,' and, 'We'll take you in now.' But he was living in anticipation of Loan Redemption Day, the day the state would settle up with him and the faith that dwelt within him had permeated his entire organism and was capable of destroying bastions of deceit, digesting poisonous toxins, halting imminent death in its tracks, and he was certain that a faith inseparable from blood, that had become one of its very components, a faith that had not abandoned him in twenty years, could not prove false, and he yelled out, 'Bugger you!' and he yelled, 'I'll be buggered if I'll go to any blasted hospital! Can you understand that?' and he yelled, 'Bloody well bugger off out of it you bastards, you damned stupid little girls!' And afterwards, when they had put away the syringes and the ampoules in their medical bags and were leaving, he had squinted at grandmother through narrow inflamed eyes and yelled, 'If I go to hospital you'll be in under the mattress quick as a flash, eh?' and delighting in his own perspicacity, he yelled in satisfaction, 'Isn't that right?' and he yelled, 'Bugger you all, there'll be no hospital for me!' But all of these memories faded in the face of one which pursued him relentlessly from that day on, entirely displacing Loan Redemption Day and occupying its former place in his mind. On his way back home through the blinding-white snow, he thought: Oh God, Oh God, Oh God, as he remembered how one autumn night three years ago he had wandered through his neighbour's house in the dark without a candle or a lantern, stumbling into corners and walls that had absorbed the oppressive smell of carbolic acid, rummaging through the cupboards, tables, beds and trunks in search of bond certificates for the unredeemed loan, sometimes coming across crockery, sometimes ancient, dusty junk, while there on the table in the middle of the large room stood the coffin holding the master of the house, his only friend, who had died the day before, and obeying an instinctive urge to vindicate the state, an urge to demonstrate his loyalty, he had muttered in the darkness, 'It's your own fault for not living long enough,' and he had muttered, 'You were told they'd pay after twenty years, but you went and died too soon, so you've only yourself to blame.' But in the depths of his soul he realized that the state was just like an earthquake, it had no need of vindication, because he saw the state as just one more force of nature, having nothing in common with living human beings, and if the state destroyed, killed and imprisoned, then it was nature that was destroying, killing and imprisoning, it was like an eclipse, like a rockslide, like the full moon, like the rain. And he thought: But I need an excuse, and he thought: But I have one. And he jabbered into the darkness, 'Everything I'm doing now is right, after all, I was the one who gave you back your memory, these bonds could have been mine even if you hadn't died, I was with you that night on the road and I was the first to see the ball lightning over the maize field and I pointed it out to you straight away, I told you it had sensed us and I told you not to budge until it drifted back to the pine forest, they all come out of the pine trees and that's the best place for them to die, but you didn't listen to me, you took to your heels and it overtook you, and it's a good thing it didn't touch you, but just hung over you. It was only the effect of it being so close that knocked you down, and that night it was me who pulled your tongue out of your throat after you swallowed it, and I gave you back your memory, without me you wouldn't even have found your own house, because you'd forgotten absolutely everything, and of course I didn't have to remind you about the bonds, but I did remind you, so what am I supposed to do now, where should I look for them now?' And he only had the one night to search, the night he'd won by spending two days persuading people there was no need to send a telegram to the dead man's only distant living relative, who lived at the other end of the world. He told them, 'She won't come anyway,' and he said, 'He was my friend, mine. Can you understand that?' and he said, 'I'll bury him myself' and, 'They'll help me,' but to himself he was thinking: If I just had one night, just one. The fear had made his bones soft on the inside, as though there was mercury enclosed in the labyrinth of bone, but charged with the cold fury of the autumn stars he had ransacked the house with a maniacal stubbornness, guided not so much by his desires as some higher, supernatural duty, opening the doors of rooms and cupboards at random, pulling out drawers, tossing aside blankets, rummaging in a trunk, sneezing in the naphtha dust, stepping in the darkness between phantom figures born of the smell of carbolic and lifeless matter, the smell of fresh planks and timber resin, knowing that if he didn't find the bonds today he wouldn't be able to continue his search tomorrow, because after the funeral the house would become the property of the village council and then of its new owner. And he didn't find them. And now as his feet sank deep into the snow on his way home, blinded by the sparkling brilliance, he thought: God almighty! and he thought: Who could have known that before he died that shithead would hang his bonds on a nail in his privy and the new owner would wipe his backside without even looking and only look afterwards, and as he remembered he thought: God almighty! God almighty!

He returned home changed in appearance, but in his gait, the set of his head, the gleam of menace in his omnipresent, watchful eyes they glimpsed his former ways and they realized that

inside he was still unchanged and not burnt out, like the wick of
a candle under the wax, even though it seemed inevitable after
what had happened that he should have burned out rapidly, for
the faith that had now been desecrated had been the inflexible
core of his being.

He no longer believed in the big state, but that in no way prevented him from believing devoutly in the little one, proof of
which was provided by the ever more frequent vile tricks with
which he finally and completely broke down grandmother, who
was three years younger than him, but lacked even the minutest
particle of the demonic fury that had nurtured and nourished
his spirit and compelled him to resist the process of ageing. She
had given him eleven children and as a consequence of women's
ailments, compounded by heavy, exhausting physical labour,
for five or six years now she had suffered from unrelenting
attacks of severe pain which made it impossible for her to sit or
lie down, so that she had to keep moving constantly. In addition
to that, she was afflicted with galloping senile dementia: she
remembered faces, but not names, she remembered fruits but
not trees, she remembered numbers but not their values, she
remembered dates but not events. Out of deep-rooted habit she
concealed the pain that had engulfed her body; terrified of doctors, she moved through this dark, altered world of unstable and
unreliable objects, groping for solid support while her old blood
washed the bits of decayed memory out of her brain and her
memories were lost, dissolved in innumerable capillaries, so
that for a while she was able to remember with her skin.
Refusing to let anything be done for her, she came close to
losing her reason completely from the savage pain in her toes,
until their last daughter but one came from Moscow and forced
her mother to let her clip off the tangled and petrified toenails
that prevented her from walking with secateurs. But soon the

unceasing movement and lack of sleep had displaced everything except the state of oblivion.

There were days when Krainov was visited by doubts and
vague premonitions, something which had almost never happened before. On those days he spent more and more time
sitting in the holy corner under the glass-covered icon, sensing
the light touch of a cobweb and the presence of the wall with the
back of his head, leaning his shoulder against the tall sturdy
shelves of light-coloured wood, on which three neatly arranged
boxes held letters, photographs, telegrams and important documents certifying his identity and everything that his identity
had been obliged to suffer, learn or accept; and also the sweet
boxes containing all the unfulfilled written promises issued by
the authorities, the empty fruit-drop tins in which the certificates of excellence were kept, together with threads and needles
and buttons that had been torn off long ago. Sometimes he
would remember about grandmother, who wandered slowly
round the house, enveloped in eternal oblivion, holding on to
the walls, incapable of sitting or lying down, always somewhere
in his field of vision, like his own eyelashes, like part of his
nose; and he would think: If you remember them, you always
see them, but if you don't remember them, it's like they don't
exist. He heard the knocking of the Mother of All Children's
wooden leg and he thought: I can hear the knocking if I listen
for it, but I can forget about it, like the beating of my heart, like
the pulsing of my blood, then it's like it doesn't exist. From time
to time he would raise his head to address the portraits of his
children hanging on three walls, issuing brusque, precise orders,
confident that they would all be carried out, if not today then
tomorrow, but sometimes he repeated himself and he felt
ashamed. And between the orders he would tell the portraits,
'The foundations of the world may collapse, but we'll survive

and only the destruction of the Earth means final and complete death,' and then he would say, 'But there'll still be someone left,' and he said, 'Only it won't be us. It'll be some other tribe.'

Nobody was surprised when he failed to pay the subscription for his shotgun the year after the redemption period for the state loan bonds expired, but they were surprised that nothing happened as a result and nobody came to confiscate his weapon. The accumulated wax of his silence and alienation continued building up in ever-thicker layers. They only came a year later, on the twenty-eighth of September, ready to stick their membership cards under his nose at the first word of protest, and the Mother of All Children went out to tell them that he wasn't at home, but he took the gun down from the wall, stood at the window for a minute, then extracted five roubles from the neglected holy corner, stuffed them into the breast pocket of his check shirt with stiff, unbending fingers and went out slowly to meet them, trying to buy time for thought, still not sure what to surrender to them, and he didn't know until the very last step, but then the thought came that his hands should make the choice for themselves, and when he stopped in front of them, his eyes fixed on the pine forest in the distance, slowly, without trembling, his hands held out the gun.